THE
ROMAN
QUESTS
ESCAPE FROM ROME

Also by Caroline Lawrence

THE ROMAN QUESTS

ESCAPE FROM ROME

Caroline Lawrence

Orion
Children's Books

Orion Children's Books

First published in Great Britain in 2016 by Hodder and Stoughton

1 3 5 7 9 10 8 6 4 2

Text copyright © Roman Mysteries Ltd 2016
Map and illustrations copyright © Richard Russell Lawrence 2016

The moral rights of the author and illustrator have been asserted.

A CIP catalogue record for this book
is available from the British Library.

ISBN: 978 1 5101 0023 7

Typeset by Input Data Services Ltd, Bridgwater, Somerset

Printed and bound in Great Britain by Clays Ltd, St Ives plc

The paper and board used in this book are
made from wood from responsible sources.

MIX
Paper from
responsible sources
FSC® C104740
www.fsc.org

Orion Children's Books
An imprint of
Hachette Children's Group
Part of Hodder and Stoughton
Carmelite House
50 Victoria Embankment
London EC4Y 0DZ

An Hachette UK Company

www.hachette.co.uk
www.hachettechildrens.co.uk

To Michael Binns, Steven Cockings
and Bronwen Riley with thanks
for their expert advice

BRITANNIA

LONDINIUM

RUTUPIAE

OCEANUS

GALLIA

MASSILIA

HISPANIA

BAELO
CLAUDIA

MARE INTERNUM

PILLARS OF
HERCULES

AFRICA

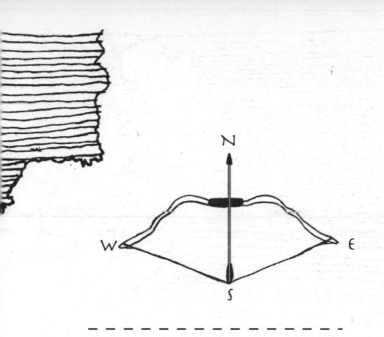

ROUTE OF THE MERCHANT SHIP CENTAUR

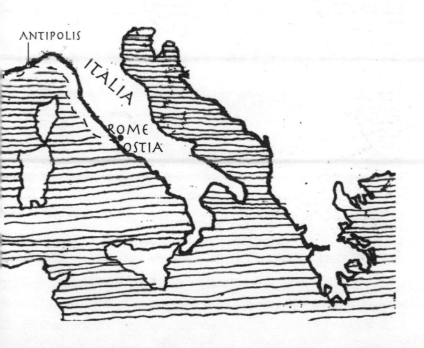

ANTIPOLIS

ITALIA

ROME
OSTIA

Salve (hello)!

Welcome to the first *Roman Quest*.

This story takes place in the ancient Roman Empire during the final years of the Emperor Domitian in the year 94 AD.

Some of the places in the story are sites that you can still visit today.

The main ones are Rome, *Ostia Antica*, *Londinium* (London) and *Fishbrook* (Fishbourne Roman Palace).

To learn more about the time and place the book is set, look at the chapter headers. Or turn to the back of the book to see what the Latin words tell us about the world of Juba and his brother and sisters.

Vale (farewell)!

Caroline

I

Chapter One
BIRRUS

The Emperor's men came at midnight.

Juba heard the banging on the distant front door as his mother shook him awake.

'Juba!' she cried. 'You have to leave. Now!'

In the flickering light of a bronze oil-lamp he could see that she was wearing his father's winter cloak even though it was a warm summer's night. Her tawny hair – the same colour as the cloak – was loose, making her seem much younger than her thirty-three years. She pulled off Juba's sheet, helped him sit up and thrust his baby sister into his arms.

Baby Dora was fast asleep, wrapped in his mother's blue palla.

'What's happening?' he yawned.

His mother quickly fastened his best leather travelling belt around his waist, then knelt to put on his boots.

'Why are you putting on my boots?' He looked around groggily. 'Where's Tutianus?'

'The slaves have gone,' she said, standing up.

'Gone? Where?'

'Away. And you must, too.' She pressed something into his hand. At first he thought it was a clay oil-lamp, then he saw that it was an ampulla: a baby's feeding bottle. It was made of

1

black-glazed clay and was decorated with a grinning actor's mask to keep away evil. The nozzle end and the filling end were both sealed with beeswax, but he could still smell milk. It was full, and heavy in his hand.

He stared at it stupidly. 'I don't understand. Why are you giving me Dora's feeding bottle?'

'Because I can't go with you.' His mother took the ampulla and put it into the neck of his tunic so that it slipped down and was caught where the belt cinched his waist. 'Keep it there,' she said. 'Your body will help it stay warm.' Then she took the tawny cloak from her shoulders and put it on him. 'This is your father's birrus Britannicus, worth a fortune. He told you its secret, didn't he?'

Juba nodded. His father had told him it was from a province called Britannia at the edge of the known world.

'Good. And do you remember who gave it to him?'

Juba nodded. 'Uncle Pantera. He brought it from Britannia.'

'Which is where you must go,' she said. He could feel her fingers trembling as she fastened the boxwood toggle at the neck and another crash came from the front door, two courtyards away.

He frowned. 'What do you mean? Where must we go? I don't understand what's happening.'

'The Emperor Domitian is taking possession of our house and everything in it. Your father and I will stay here and distract his men long enough for you to escape.'

'Escape?' Juba wondered if this was all a strange dream.

But he knew it wasn't when she took his shoulders and shook him. 'Juba, listen! Someone has denounced us. Do you know what that means?'

Juba nodded. His tutor Serapion had been teaching them

about Roman law. 'It's when an informer – a delator – accuses someone of treason against the Emperor and takes them to court. If he wins his case then he confiscates the traitor's property and divides it with the Emperor.'

She nodded. 'And the delator always wins because the Emperor always gains. Juba, someone has denounced us. Your father and I will stay behind to divert the Emperor's guards so you can take Fronto and your sisters as far from Rome as possible. Go to your uncle Pantera in Britannia. He has a seaside villa near a town called Londinium. Here!' She reached behind her neck and took off her necklace.

'Your Minerva cameo!' He stared at the gem on its gold chain. Carved in four different coloured layers of sardonyx, it showed the goddess in profile. 'But it's worth a fortune!'

'No, Juba. It is worth four fortunes. One for each of you. The money you raise from its sale should buy your passage to Britannia, with enough left over to get you to your uncle's villa.' She tucked the cameo out of sight in the neck of his tunic. 'I've also put gold in your belt pouch. When you get to Ostia, buy a slave girl who can nurse the baby.'

'Buy a slave girl?' he stared at her.

'Yes! Take her with you on the ship to Britannia. If you can't find a wet nurse, a goat will do. If all that isn't enough you have everything you need right here.' She patted his chest. 'Do you understand?'

He stared down at his baby sister. Small but solid, with creamy brown skin and silky black curls, she was already very beautiful.

A distant splintering crash told Juba that the front door had finally been broken. He heard his father's voice, deep and angry. His mother's cold hands on his cheeks brought Juba's head

3

round so that she could look him in the eye. He could see she was fighting tears.

'Juba. Your brother is older but you know he's . . . different. You have to be a brave leader, like your hero Aeneas. Promise me you will do everything in your power to save the children.'

Juba felt sick, but he took a deep breath and nodded. 'I promise,' he said, feeling the weight of his baby sister in his arms.

His mother kissed his forehead. 'Farewell, my son. I love you.' Then she pushed him through the curtained doorway and into the courtyard.

Chapter Two
LUCERNA

Fourteen-year-old Fronto was dreaming about the Trojan Horse when his younger brother Juba shook him awake.

'Fronto! Get up!' cried Juba.

Fronto blinked. 'Is it still night? I was dreaming about the sack of Troy.'

'We have to go now! Put on your best tunic and cloak.'

Fronto looked around. 'Where's Jucundus?'

'You have to get ready without your slave.'

Fronto folded his arms across his chest. Getting up in the middle of the night was wrong. Getting dressed without the help of his slave was worse.

'It's a game!' Juba said. He was holding their baby sister. 'We're playing *Escape from Troy*. We're the Trojans. The Greeks have come out of the hollow horse to get us.'

Fronto pondered this, and then unfolded his arms. 'All right,' he said at last. 'I like games.' He went to the cedarwood chest at the foot of his bed, opened it and pulled out a cherry-coloured tunic. 'I'll wear this one,' he said. 'It's my lucky tunic.'

'Take your lucky cloak, too. And your boots, not your sandals.'

Fronto took his dark brown hooded cloak from its peg, then

fished under his bed for his boots. 'Why are you wearing father's birrus Britannicus?'

'Because it's the colour of a lion skin,' Juba said. 'Remember Aeneas wore a lion skin like Hercules when he took his family from burning Troy?'

'Of course I remember,' Fronto said. He pulled on his right boot, then stopped and looked at Juba. 'Does that mean you get to be the hero, Aeneas?'

'Yes!' Juba hissed. 'Just put on your other boot.'

From another part of the house came a crash, and then shouting.

'What was that?' asked Fronto in alarm.

'Pater and Mater are playing, too,' Juba said. 'They're pretending to be the Greeks, coming out of the Trojan horse.

'Oh!' Fronto said.

His brother pushed him towards the inner door that led to their sister's room next door.

Even though it was just a game, Fronto touched the door frame at shoulder level three times for good luck: *right, left, right*.

His sister Domitia Ursula was already awake and sitting up in bed. She had the darkest skin of the four of them, so at first all Fronto could see were her catlike eyes, made green by the yellow flame of a small oil-lamp.

'Ursula!' whispered Juba. 'We're playing *Escape from Troy*. Get dressed.'

'But it's night-time,' Ursula said, hugging a toy puppy made of rabbit fur stuffed with wool. 'And I heard strange noises.'

'Don't worry,' Fronto said. 'It's just a game.'

Juba nodded. 'Like the time Pater and Mater pretended the house was on fire to see how we would cope.'

Ursula narrowed her eyes at them and made no move to get up.

'Listen,' Juba said to Ursula. 'Pater said they'll get us each a puppy if we can get all the way to the Ostia Gate without anybody seeing us.'

'A real puppy?' breathed Ursula. 'Not a rabbit fur one like Canicula?' She held up her soft toy.

Juba nodded and Fronto grinned as his younger sister leapt out of bed. For years she had been begging their parents for a real puppy.

As Ursula dressed she asked, 'Can I bring Loquax? I would bring him if it was a real emergency.'

'All right,' Juba whispered. 'But keep him in his cage, and quiet. And be quick!'

Ursula hurriedly tied the belt of her tunic and stepped up onto an elephant-shaped ebony stool to take the wicker birdcage down from its hook. The cage was covered with a dark blue linen cloth. This showed the bird it was night, and time to be quiet.

The elephant stool wobbled and she almost fell. But she recovered her balance and jumped down lightly, holding the covered cage.

Juba took a deep breath. 'Put on your winter cloak please, Ursula,' he said. 'And boots.'

As Ursula tugged on her boots, Juba went to the outer door of her bedroom, pulled back the curtain a finger's width and peeped out.

'Blow out the lamp!' he hissed at Fronto.

Fronto obediently blew out the gilded bronze oil-lamp on Ursula's bedside table. They were plunged into darkness.

Silvery moonlight washed the room as Juba pulled the

tapestry curtain back. 'Now!' he hissed. 'Along the colonnade and into the storeroom. Quick as you can!'

Fronto rapidly touched each side of the doorframe – *right, left, right* – then tiptoed along the walkway towards the storeroom and slave-quarters.

Even though he knew it was a game, his heart was thudding against his ribs.

Fronto grinned. This was exciting!

Chapter Three
AMPHORAE

Juba closed the storeroom door behind them and pressed his back against it. It was solid, but there was no bolt on the inside. He hugged his baby sister and tried to think.

Even though it was dark, he closed his eyes because it helped him concentrate.

He knew that wheels of cheese and bunches of herbs hung from the ceiling, and a whole side of dried beef that had been part payment for a pearl necklace.

On his right, two dozen amphorae full of the finest wine and olive oil leaned against the wall. In the far corner were pieces of old furniture and some equipment belonging to builders who had decorated the triclinium wall.

To his left was a door that led to the slave quarters.

And straight ahead of him was their only chance of escape: a door that opened onto a narrow back alley and from there the streets of Rome.

'Do we really need to bring the baby?' whispered Ursula.

Juba nodded and opened his eyes.

'Then let me use Mater's palla to strap her to my body,' offered Ursula. 'I know how.'

'All right, but hurry!' Juba hissed.

As Fronto helped his sister strap on the baby, Juba tiptoed forward to peep in the slave quarters.

A burning torch in a wall bracket showed him a dozen empty stalls in a vaulted tunnel. He had not been here for years, since he was a toddler, and he was surprised to see how cramped they were.

He pulled the wooden door closed so his brother and sister would not notice that the slaves were gone.

'Shhh!' he lied. 'The slaves are all asleep. Let's be as quiet as we can.'

With trembling hands, he lifted the wooden bar of the back door. It would fall back into place once they were outside.

Juba winced as the iron door hinge squeaked in its marble socket.

He hesitated. He had never been on the streets of Rome without his parents or a bodyguard, especially not at night. He knew it was a dangerous place, full of beggars, criminals, disease and death. He had a superstitious brother, a feisty sister and a baby who might start crying at any moment. How would he ever get them all to safety?

Then he heard an ominous thump on the other side of the storeroom door, and low male voices. It was the Emperor's henchmen.

'Come on,' he hissed. 'Let's go!'

Chapter Four
AENEAS

They were about two blocks from home, heading down the dark streets of the Palatine Hill, when Juba felt a tug at his cloak.

He whirled round to see it was only his brother. 'By the gods, Fronto!' he gasped. 'Don't do that. What do you want, anyway?'

'You have to carry me on your back!'

'I *what?*'

'You have to carry me on your back!' Fronto repeated. 'Remember how Aeneas had to carry his father on his back when they fled burning Troy?'

'Of course,' Juba said. 'Like the silver statue Pater used to have in his study.'

'Yes! If you get to be the hero, then I get to be his father. Carry me!'

His voice was loud, too loud.

Juba glanced at the dark streets behind them: the Emperor's men might appear any minute. *Play the game*, he told himself.

'All right!' he muttered. 'But just to the bottom of the hill.' He turned his back to Fronto and bent forward. 'By Jupiter!' he gasped as his brother climbed aboard. 'You're heavy. Wait! Not so tight. You're choking me!'

Fronto loosened his grasp. 'Now you know what Aeneas felt like!' he laughed.

Juba started to stagger down the hill. 'Poor Aeneas,' he grunted.

With every step he felt his stomach clench. He was running away like a coward.

When they reached a quiet place where an aqueduct passed overhead Juba could no longer bear his brother's weight. Or his guilt. He let his brother down and looked around, breathing hard. Houses were built against and under the aqueduct. At the places where its supporting arches met the walls they cast inky black shadows.

Juba led them under one of these shadowed arches.

'What are we doing here?' Ursula asked.

'I just remembered something important,' Juba whispered. 'If this was a real emergency we would need to bring our household gods for protection. I'm going back to get them. You and Fronto wait here under this arch. With your dark cloaks, I can hardly see you there. If you don't move and don't peep, you'll be safe. Oh, and if the baby wakes, give her this.'

He reached into the neck of his tunic, brought out Dora's feeding bottle and handed it to Ursula.

She frowned at it. 'This is a stupid game,' she said. 'I want to go home.'

'Do you want a puppy?'

She put down the bird-cage and took the bottle.

'If she gets a puppy, can I have a horse?' asked Fronto.

'Yes,' said Juba. 'I'm sure Pater and Mater will let you have a horse.'

He left before they could protest any more, keeping to the darkest shadows on the side of the road.

Please help me be brave, father Jupiter, he prayed. *Please help me be brave.*

As he hurried back up the dark streets he tried to muster his courage by resting his hand on the ivory handle of his dagger.

He had only seen two soldiers searching the house. Maybe with the element of surprise he could help his parents get away from them.

His father was very rich, with enough gold and jewels to buy ships, houses and slaves. If he could help his parents escape, then the six of them could sail anywhere in the Empire. To Britannia. Or Alexandria. Maybe even to Asia, the homeland of Aeneas.

When he reached his own street he looked round the corner. For a heartbeat he thought all was well. The double doors were wide open, as if to welcome his father's clients on a dark winter morning. He could see the silhouettes of their two door-slaves either side of the door.

Then he looked again. The two figures were not their door-slaves; they were soldiers wearing the white-crested helmets of the Praetorian Guard, the Emperor's personal bodyguard.

And the double doors were not open, they were shattered.

Juba shrank back round the corner, his heart pounding furiously. Earlier, peering out of Ursula's room, he had seen a short soldier with a squashed nose and a tall one with a hooked nose. The two by the door were younger and more muscular. That meant there were at least four of them, maybe more.

It was so quiet that Juba could hear his heart thudding. The houses around his were silent. No shutter squeaked open. No watchdog barked. Only the cicadas creaked faintly. The shouts and banging must have woken his neighbours but they were probably cowering in their homes, afraid that they might suffer the same fate as his family.

Juba felt a sickening plunge of his stomach: he knew that if he called for help, nobody would come. He was on his own.

Through the doorway he could see his atrium. It was so brightly lit by torches that he could even make out the household shrine in the far corner. The shrine was a miniature wooden temple on top of a cabinet. The cabinet itself contained silverware and other treasures, and a secret panel with his father's most precious jewels.

Inside the model temple on top of the cabinet were offerings of fruit, small cakes and charred pinecones. Painted on the back panel were two lucky snakes and two youths with fluttering tunics.

Most important of all were the three little statues of Jupiter, Mercury and Venus. They were his family's special household gods. His father prayed to them every morning and burned incense to them on special days. And his mother always took them on their trips to Naples and back.

The three figurines were still in the shrine, which meant his parents had not got away. They would need his help.

He was mustering his courage when a crash followed by shouts came from within the depths of his house.

The two guards looked at each other, then turned and went inside.

Juba watched them go through his atrium, past the household shrine and down the corridor that led to the fountain courtyard. A thought occurred to him: if the gems inside the shrine were gone, that might mean his parents were safe.

If not, they would need them when they met up again in Britannia.

Before his courage could fail, Juba ran forward, his tawny cloak flapping behind him. He hid behind one of the columns of the porch. Its painted plaster was chalky on the sweaty palms of his hands. Hearing nothing, he crossed the threshold into the bright atrium and crouched in front of the shrine.

As quickly and quietly as he could, he opened the cabinet doors. Five life-sized wax faces swung on their nails, two on the left, three on the right. The death masks of his ancestors seemed to be shaking their heads at him. Their empty eye sockets looked spooky in the torchlight.

'Sorry,' he whispered and made the sign against evil.

Groping in the depths of the cabinet, his fingertips found the secret panel and felt it fall.

His father kept his best specimens in a flat ebony box: dark green emeralds, light green jasper, purple amethyst, apricot-coloured sardonyx and a pale pink pearl the size of a chickpea. That pearl was the most valuable thing he owned.

After you children and your mother, his father had told them, *The Pearl of Iris is my most valuable possession. In the time of Julius Caesar it was sold for ten million sesterces. It is worth more than both our houses and everything in them.*

The box was there, but it was empty.

He felt a huge wave of relief wash over him. *Good*, he told himself. *Pater and Mater must have the jewels.*

He was gathering up the three household gods when the sound of men's voices and the crunch of boots sent a jolt of panic racing through his body.

He had been a fool to return. If the Emperor's henchmen caught him, Fronto and his sisters would be helpless. They thought they were playing a game. They didn't know their lives really were in danger. They had no idea who was after them or where they should be going.

Juba looked frantically for a place to hide. The porter's alcove had a painted screen that hid his bench from view.

Juba ran to it.

But when he slid behind the screen, he saw a sight that would haunt him for the rest of his life.

Chapter Five
AQUAE DUCTUM

U rsula knew she was braver than both her brothers.

When she was six she had crept out of the house to watch half-naked boys dressed in goatskin run down the streets for the festival of Lupercalia. When she was seven she had accepted a slave boy's dare to scramble up the new grape vine trellis to the roof of their townhouse. Then last year, aged eight, she had been the only one brave enough to pick up the strange black bird with the yellow beak and broken wing. The poor thing had flown into one of the marble discs that hung between the columns of their inner rose garden. She had nursed him back to health, enduring his frightened pecks and flapping. She had not even been scared the first time the bird spoke to her in a strangely human voice, saying '*Ave, Domitian!*' She had named the bird Loquax and he was her dearest companion.

Now, hiding under the big arch of the aqueduct with her elder brother and baby sister, Ursula was not scared. She was furious.

She knew Juba was pretending to play a game. But he should trust her enough to tell her the truth and not try to bribe her with the false promise of a puppy.

And now he had disappeared into the night. What if he never

17

came back? She did not even know what they were running from. Or where they were really going. And he had left baby Dora with her.

Ursula hated the feeling of not being in control. It made her angry, like a wild animal in a cage. She wanted to scream in frustration. Or hit something. Unable to stay still, she thrust Loquax's cage into Fronto's surprised arms and began to pace back and forth in front of the arch, stroking her baby sister's back.

'Ursula!' hissed Fronto. 'Juba told us to wait here in the shadows.'

The faint slap of running feet on paving stones made her freeze.

Was Juba coming back already?

Yes!

She recognised his tawny cloak as he skidded round a corner.

'Run!' he gasped. 'They're after me!'

Fronto laughed and, still clutching Loquax's cage, he charged after his brother.

But Ursula had caught a glimpse of Juba's face in the moonlight.

She knew for sure that it was not a game.

Clutching baby Dora tight, she ran too.

And for the first time that night she was more afraid than angry.

Chapter Six
CIRCUS MAXIMUS

As Juba pounded past the curved southern end of the Circus Maximus, the dark streets grew brighter and more crowded. He could smell spices from the great warehouses by the river and he could hear the sound of whip-cracks and wagon wheels. They were getting close to the busy Ostia Gate.

Carts and carriages were not allowed in the city of Rome in daylight hours, so all deliveries had to be at night.

Juba slowed his pace and jogged gratefully between fast-moving men and slow-moving beasts.

But his chest was still heaving and sweat was pouring down his body as he finally came to a stop in a shadowed doorway near some stables. Fronto ran up a few moments later, still hugging the cloth-covered birdcage. Torchlight showed his face shiny with sweat; like Juba, he was wearing a winter cloak.

'Gods!' gasped Fronto, touching the doorway three times: *right, left, right*. 'I don't think . . . I've ever run . . . so fast . . . in my life. That was good.'

'Get back!' Juba pulled his brother into the shadow of the doorway, then looked over Fronto's shoulder into the crowd of people moving along the pavement.

'Where's Ursula?' he asked. 'Isn't she with you?'

'She'll be here . . . soon,' gasped Fronto. 'She's a better . . . runner . . . than either of us!'

'But she was carrying Dora!' cried Juba. 'And she's only nine. She'll get lost in the crowds!'

'She'll be here!' Fronto repeated. Again and again, he touched the sides of the doorway for good luck.

But by the time Juba's heartbeat had returned to normal, there was still no sign of Ursula and the night-time crowds were thicker than ever.

'When did you last see her?' Juba asked Fronto.

'Not sure,' said his older brother. 'By the Circus Maximus, I think.'

'*Jupiter, protect her from the Emperor's men,*' prayed Juba. Then to Fronto, 'Wait inside that stable.'

'To choose my horse?'

'Yes!' lied Juba. 'But we're not at the gate yet, so if you see any soldiers, hide!'

'Did Mater and Pater hire actors?' Fronto asked. 'Like at their party?'

'Yes!' Juba lied again. 'And if they find us then we lose the game. So get inside!'

He watched his brother go a few paces, step round a pile of steaming manure and then disappear into the large open door of the stable.

Then, with another prayer, he set back the way he had come.

He looked down dark alleys and behind splashing fountains. He felt dizzy and sick. *Both his sisters were gone!*

His mother had asked one thing of him: to save the children. And he had failed.

Fronto had last seen Ursula outside Rome's great racecourse, the Circus Maximus, so Juba spent extra time looking under the dark arches. There were other people there: beggars sleeping and a couple kissing. But no Ursula.

He was just about to admit defeat when he heard the faint sound of a kitten mewing and found his sister crouching in the shadows of an umbrella pine a stone's throw from the racecourse.

'Ursula,' he cried, relief washing over him. 'What in Hades are you doing?'

'I found a kitten!' She looked up at him with shining eyes. 'Their mother was gone and all her brothers and sisters were dead. But look! She's alive!'

'*Meeer!*' said the tiny creature in Ursula's arms. '*Meeer!*'

Then the kitten grew silent.

'At last!' cried Ursula. 'She's feeding!'

With horror, Juba saw that she was using baby Dora's ceramic bottle to feed the kitten milk.

'What are you doing!' hissed Juba. 'That milk is for Dora, not for some stray kitten.'

'She's only tiny,' Ursula said. 'She won't drink much. And Dora usually sleeps through the night. This milk is just to comfort her if she wakes.'

Juba squatted. 'Ursula,' he said. 'You're very brave so I can tell you. This is not a game. We are running for our lives.'

She glanced up at him. 'I know that,' she said. 'But how could I pass by a poor orphaned kitten? And look! She's had enough.' Ursula pressed the blobs of wax back on the two open ends of the ceramic baby feeder and slipped it down the front of her tunic. She stretched out her arm. 'Help me up,' she said. 'Meer and Dora and I are ready to go now.'

'Meer?' Juba said. 'Who's Meer?'

'My kitten! She told me her name.'

Juba swallowed hard. His sister's courage and compassion shamed him.

He held out his hand. 'Come on, then,' he said, pulling her to her feet. 'With Meer the kitten on our side we can't fail.'

Chapter Seven
PORTA OSTIENSIS

Fronto liked the stables. They were quiet and dark and smelled of sweet hay and horses. Many things made him panic, but horses made him feel strangely calm.

He had chosen a fine bay stallion with liquid black eyes and a black mane. He would call it Ammon after his special god, Jupiter Ammon.

Meanwhile, he had been touching all the stall doors – *right, left, right* – to ensure Ursula's safety. He had just reached the last one when Juba appeared with his sister.

'Thank you, Jupiter Ammon!' Fronto whispered, and ran to them. 'I've just chosen my horse,' he said, excited.

In the quiet of the dim space, Juba said, 'Pater told me you can choose your horse when we reach Ostia.'

'Ostia the seaport?' Fronto frowned.

'Yes.'

Fronto was confused. 'But Ostia is fifteen miles from here.'

'It's part of the challenge,' said Juba.

'But that means we have to go out of the gate,' Fronto said. 'We have to leave the protection of Rome's town walls!'

'Don't worry,' Juba reached into the neck of his tunic. 'I brought the household gods to protect us. Here. You take Jupiter

Ammon. Ursula has the ivory Venus and I have Mercury.'

Fronto took the small bronze statuette of Jupiter Ammon and admired it. It showed the king of the gods with ram's horns rising from his forehead and curling round his ears. The god's face looked brave and calm. 'Help me do this, Jupiter Ammon,' Fronto whispered. The statuette of the god comforted him, but his heart was still pounding as he followed his brother out of the stables towards the gate in the town wall.

As the three of them drew closer to the marble arch, he had to tip his head further back to look at it. If he hadn't been holding the birdcage, he would have put his fingers in his ears: this part of Rome was almost as noisy at night as it was in the daytime. Maybe even noisier.

The grinding of iron-rimmed wheels on the stone street, whips cracking and drivers shouting mixed with the sound of braying mules, shouting stall-holders, laughing women, pleading beggars and jingling worshippers of the goddess Isis.

Someone even lifted up the cloth on Loquax's cage to peek underneath and Ursula's bird squawked *'Ave, Domitian! What ARE you doing!'*

The sounds went into Fronto's ears and made his nerves jangle like a tambourine. But he gritted his teeth and when they reached the arch he skipped across the broad marble threshold, leading with his right foot and bringing his left up to meet it. He held the birdcage in his left hand and with his right he touched the marble side of the arch: *right, left, right.*

Fronto knew if he made a mistake he would have to go back and do it again.

Thankfully, he did it right.

Once outside the town walls, the world was suddenly quieter. He could still hear grinding wheels, whip cracks and a mule's bray, but the sounds were fainter in the vast outdoors. He made the sign against evil for they were now in the necropolis, the 'city of the dead'.

A sinking half moon shone on a white marble pyramid. Fronto knew it was the tomb of a man named Cestius and one of the great landmarks that showed travellers from Ostia that they had reached Rome. Beyond it were many house-shaped tombs and behind them, on his right, loomed Potsherd Mountain. This was a huge mound of broken amphora pieces that gave off the stench of rancid olive oil. He could smell the river, too, though he could not see it.

A steady stream of oxcarts and mule-drawn wagons moved both ways in the centre of the road while pedestrians used a bare earthen track on either side.

Fronto noticed that some of the carts going back towards Ostia were empty. One passed so slowly he was able to quickly touch its wooden side: *right, left, right.*

'The baby's wet,' Ursula said. 'I'd better see to her.'

'Not right here,' said Juba, glancing around. 'Let's go behind that mausoleum.'

While Ursula and Juba were changing the baby, Fronto wandered off to look at some smaller tombs further back from the road. The moonlight was just bright enough to let him read some of the inscriptions.

One marble stone told of a nine-year-old boy named Anthus crushed by the wheels of an oxcart. Fronto touched the red-painted inscription three times for good luck. Turning to go back, he saw four figures sitting around a fire deeper in the necropolis.

Hurrying back to his brother and sisters by a different route, he passed a big house-shaped tomb that looked oddly familiar.

25

It had red clay roof tiles and a marble palmette at the front where the roof peaked. He could just make out the inscription above the door. He read it out loud, as he always did.

L. DOMITIUS AFRICANUS, FREEDMAN OF THE EMPEROR NERO, MADE THIS FOR HIMSELF AND HIS DESCENDANTS.

Fronto clapped his hands.

'Juba! Ursula!' he cried. 'Come quick! I've just found our tomb!'

Chapter Eight
NECROPOLIS

Juba stood in front of the marble tomb. His family came here every year to observe the Parentalia, the festival commemorating dead ancestors. In mid February, when the first trees were in blossom and the sun was bright and fresh, they would bring gifts of salt, bread, wine and garlands. Tonight, in the faint moonlight, it looked very different. The white marble seemed cold, and the red roof tiles blood red. Behind the locked door were urns filled with ashes of the dead.

Remembering what he had seen in his atrium, Juba shuddered and made the sign against evil.

'It's not a bad omen,' Fronto said cheerfully. 'We can ask our ancestors to help us get to Ostia.' He put up the hood of his brown cloak and prayed, 'O Ancestors of our father, protect us and help us get to Ostia so Ursula can get her puppy and I can get my horse.'

Juba swallowed hard. *How much longer can I keep up this pretence?* he asked himself.

Somewhere in the flat-topped pines a nightingale let forth a sweet warble of notes.

'It's a good omen!' Fronto said. 'That nightingale song shows the gods have heard us.'

Juba patted his brother's back and started back to the main road.

They were about to emerge from between two tombs when he saw three men on horseback. The riders were passing a torchlit cart which showed their profiles, dark against the fire behind them: the short one with his squashed nose, and the taller one with a hooked nose. They were the Emperor's henchmen. And a mysterious hooded man was riding with them.

Juba threw out both arms to stop the others. 'Pull up your hoods,' he hissed. 'And be quiet.'

When the riders had passed by, Juba let out a sigh of relief. If they hadn't left the road and then stopped to pray to their ancestors, they might have been captured. Maybe the gods *were* with them.

'Those men on horseback?' said Ursula quietly. 'Were they the ones making all the noise back at the house?'

Juba nodded. 'Be quiet,' he mouthed, and glanced at Fronto. Ursula gave a small nod to show she understood.

'Who was the man with the pointy hood?' Fronto asked. 'He wasn't dressed as a soldier.'

Juba had been wondering that very thing. Could the hooded man be the evil Emperor himself? People said he sometimes disguised himself as an ordinary Roman citizen. And everyone knew how much he loved to play cruel practical jokes.

Before Juba could reply, something slammed him against the wall of the tomb with such force that the air was knocked from his lungs. He felt the cold blade of a knife at his throat.

'Give us your gold,' came a rough voice. 'Or I'll kill all three of you before you can blink.'

Chapter Nine
GEMMA

Fronto tasted sour panic as sharp metal pressed his throat. Angry hands pushed him hard against the brick wall of a tomb. Two grubby faces loomed in his field of vision and he smelled rancid wine on their breath. It took him a moment to realise they were women.

He slid his eyes to see a third woman with hair like a dirty sheep holding his sister in a wrestler's grip.

On his right, a ragged man had Juba pinned against a marble tomb.

'Give us your money,' said one of the women, her face only inches from his.

Then, baby Dora began to cry.

Fronto struggled to get free. Surely he was stronger than two beggar women?

The knife pricked his neck and he felt a trickle of warm blood. 'Don't even think about it!' she whispered. Her hands were cold and strong as iron. To the man she said, 'Got anything?'

Out of the corner of his eye, Fronto saw the man's fingers grope at the pouch on Juba's leather belt. 'Gold!' the man cried, stuffing the coins down the front of his tunic. 'And this fine gem!'

'Please!' Juba cried. 'Not the Minerva necklace!'

Dora wailed and Ursula tried to calm her.

A tug at Fronto's neck brought his attention back to the woman with the knife. 'Look!' she cried. 'This one's got a gold bulla round his neck!'

'No!' he cried. 'That protects me from bad luck!'

'Well it didn't work, did it?' She laughed and ripped it away. 'Take off that nice ring. Orange is my favourite colour, along with gold.' Her breath made him gag.

'I can't,' he gasped. 'My fingers are swollen.'

'They aren't swollen,' sneered the woman. 'They're fat. You're a plump, well-fed rich boy, aren't you? Take it off or I'll cut off your finger!'

She let go of his hands but kept his upper arms pinned against the tomb.

Fronto tried to pull off the carnelian signet ring showing Jupiter with ram's horns. But it was stuck fast.

'What's this?' The other woman had left him to pick up Loquax's cage. 'Oh, have the rich kiddies got a little songbird?' she asked in a mocking tone.

'*Ave, Domitian!*' came a strangled voice as she lifted the cloth.

The woman uttered a hoarse scream and dropped the cage.

'It's a demon!' she yelled. 'Run for it!'

Chapter Ten
DAEMON

When the robber woman dropped the cage, the wicker door popped open and Ursula's bird flew out and flapped about them with black wings.

'*Ave, Domitian!*' it cried in a spookily human voice.

With yelps of alarm, all four robbers stumbled off into the darkness, heading away from the Ostia road.

Ursula could hear Loquax pursuing them. The bird's cries grew fainter and fainter. '*Ave, Domitian! What ARE you doing?*' And finally: '*Good night!*'

'Thank you, Loquax,' Ursula breathed, and blinked back tears as she hugged Dora tight. 'You saved us.' But as she squeezed her baby sister with relief, she felt needle-sharp claws scrabble at her bare tummy. 'Ouch!' she cried. 'Ouch! Ouch! Ouch!'

'Ursula!' Juba ran to her. 'Did she stab you?'

'No!' Ursula handed him the baby and reached down the front of her tunic. 'It's the kitten in my tunic!'

She drew out the tiny brown and grey kitten.

'*Meeer!*' said the tiny creature. '*Meeer!*'

'Where on earth did that come from?' Fronto gaped.

'I found her by the Circus Maximus. She was hungry and crying for her mother.'

'So you're not hurt?' Juba asked.

'No, I'm fine. But they took Dora's good luck charm.'

'They took my bulla, too,' Fronto slumped onto the ground.

'And mine,' muttered Juba. 'But we still have our gods; they'll protect us.'

At least Dora was only whimpering now. Juba patted her back to soothe her. Ursula picked up the empty birdcage, stuffed the dark cloth inside and carefully placed the kitten among the folds.

'We'd better get out of here,' Juba said. 'Before they realise Loquax is just a talking bird and not a demon.' Then he cursed. 'Pollux! They took the Minerva Cameo. It's supposed to pay for our passage to Britannia. Help me look! Maybe they dropped it . . .' Still holding baby Dora, he started searching the moonlit weeds and grasses.

'Mater's Minerva cameo?' Fronto stared at him. 'Passage to Britannia? What are you talking about?'

Juba sighed. 'You know how we were playing *Escape from Troy*?' he said. 'Well, it's not a game. We really are running for our lives. We have to leave our fatherland and find a new home.'

'In Britannia?' Ursula said. 'But that's the edge of the world!'

'You said it was a game.' Fronto folded his arms across his chest. 'You lied.'

'I know,' said Juba. 'And I'm sorry. I only did it so you wouldn't be afraid.'

'You said we only had to get as far as Ostia. I want my horse and I want to go home.'

'Listen to me,' Juba shifted Dora in his arms. 'The men chasing us weren't actors. They were soldiers from Domitian's Praetorian Guard. Someone denounced us and the Emperor sent men to arrest us all. Mater and Pater told us to go as far away as we can. That's why we're going to Uncle Pantera in Britannia.'

'I want my horse and I want to go home,' Fronto repeated. He was tapping the nearest tomb obsessively: *right, left, right.*

Ursula looked at Juba. If he said the wrong thing then they might be here all night.

'I'm sorry Fronto,' Juba said. 'Maybe we'll be able to get you a horse in Britannia. But we can never go home again.'

Chapter Eleven
PLAUSTRUM

'It's my fault; I did it wrong. It's my fault; I did it wrong.'

Fronto had been muttering this phrase over and over while tapping the door frame of the nearest tomb with the bronze head of Jupiter Ammon: *right, left, right.*

'You didn't do anything wrong,' Juba told his brother as patiently as he could.

'I must have,' said Fronto. 'We're being chased and we've been robbed and Loquax is gone and we can't go home again. It's my fault; I did it wrong.'

'What did you do wrong?' Juba said.

'I don't know. But if I do it right, maybe I can fix it.'

Juba shifted the baby to his other arm and looked at Ursula. The moon had set, but he could see her shake her head.

They both knew from experience that Fronto could get caught up in chanting his good luck formulas for hours.

'Fronto, listen,' said Juba. 'We're alive and together. That's what counts. Come on. Before the robbers come back or the Emperor's men find us.'

Fronto kept tapping. 'Just let me finish another thousand.'

Juba felt sick. The image of what he had seen behind the screen back at his house was pressed into his memory like the stamp of

34

a signet ring on hardened wax. And he heard his mother's last words over and over: *Save the children, save the children.*

He closed his eyes and whispered a prayer, 'Help me, Father Jupiter. What would Aeneas do?'

This gave him an idea as clear as a comet streaking across a night sky.

He turned to his brother again.

'Fronto,' he said. 'When Aeneas was fleeing burning Troy, what did he do wrong?'

Fronto stopped tapping and turned to look at Juba.

'Nothing. It was his destiny to find a New Troy. And he did.'

Juba looked down at Dora, now sleeping. 'Maybe we have a destiny, too,' he said. 'Don't you see? Everything seems bleak now, but maybe it's all for a reason.'

Fronto nodded slowly. But he made no move to go.

'Fronto.' Juba held out the baby. 'You're the strongest of us. Can you take Dora for a while?'

Juba held his breath, and then exhaled in relief as his brother nodded.

'All right,' Fronto said. 'Help me strap her on.'

A tenth of an hour later they were on the way towards Ostia again.

Fronto was still muttering, but this time it was to baby Dora, 'We're alive and together. We're alive and together.'

Juba offered up a silent prayer of thanks to Jupiter Ammon.

'Well done!' Ursula whispered.

He turned his head, 'When did you get to be so brave?'

'I've always been brave. You just never noticed.'

From behind them came the distinctive clank of an oxcart bell and the grinding of iron wheel rims on the stone road.

They stood well back to avoid being crushed, but the driver

caught sight of them in the dim starlight. He slowed his cart to a stop and offered them a lift to Ostia if they would take it in turns to sit beside him and hold the reins.

Fronto climbed carefully in the back, not forgetting to tap *right, left, right*, but only once. Cradling baby Dora in her sling, he stretched out on the fish-smelling hay and fell asleep instantly. Ursula lay beside him. Juba sat beside the driver and held the reins, promising to wake Ursula in an hour.

His head was nodding when she tapped his shoulder, refreshed from a catnap and eager to take over. He collapsed beside his brother on the fishy hay in the back of the cart. The night air was chilly, so he pulled his cloak round him. At first he could feel a few hard pebbles, but when he shifted so that they didn't dig into him he fell asleep. It seemed only moments later that baby Dora started to cry.

Juba yawned and stretched, but his stretch became a shudder when he remembered what had happened.

'Hey,' said the old driver. 'You better shush that baby. My ox Hector hates the sound.'

Fronto was awake now, too. He sat up and jounced baby Dora. 'We're alive and together,' he told her, but it didn't stop her sobs.

'That's her hungry cry.' Ursula turned her head, still holding the reins.

Juba sighed. The air was damp on his face and the sky was grey. Dawn was coming. 'How much farther to Ostia?' he asked.

'You don't understand.' The driver took the reins from Ursula and tugged on them. When the noisy oxcart ground to a stop, Dora's cries seemed even louder.

The cart-driver pointed to his ox. 'See the hay tied to Hector's horns?'

36

In the grey light they could just make out some strands of hay tied to the ox's horns.

'Yes,' Juba said.

'You know what that means?'

Juba and Ursula shook their heads but Fronto said, 'I do. It means the ox is dangerous. It means he trampled someone.'

'That's right,' said the old driver. 'And what set him off that time was a baby crying. So I'll have to leave you here.'

Juba was about to protest, but when Hector rolled his eyes and snorted they scrambled off the back of the cart. The driver flicked the reins and drove off. When the rumble of iron wheels and the clank of the bell finally faded, Dora's crying seemed louder than ever.

'Let me hold her for a while,' Ursula said, handing Juba the kitten in its cage. 'Maybe I can quiet her.' She helped Fronto undo the knot of the sling and took the baby. 'She's not wet, but she's hungry.'

'Where's her feeding bottle?' Fronto asked.

'It's empty,' Ursula replied.

'Empty?' echoed Juba in horror. 'You mean you gave all her milk to your kitten?'

'No!' Ursula scowled at him. 'Meer only drank a little. I gave most of it to Dora a while ago. We just have to find someone with milk in Ostia.'

Juba sighed and nodded. 'We can't be far,' he said. 'This is the outskirts of the necropolis.'

'I think I can see the walls of the city, up ahead,' Fronto said. 'And look! See that yellow star over there? I'll bet that's the lighthouse at Portus.'

'I can't see any lighthouse,' Ursula said. 'But I see three men on white horses riding this way.' She clutched baby Dora. 'Two

37

of them are soldiers and the third has a pointy hood.'

Juba looked, and his heart seemed to leap into his throat. Even at this distance he knew it was the Emperor's men.

'Run!' he cried. 'And stay close to me!' Still holding the kitten in the birdcage, he left the road and plunged into the necropolis, weaving between the tombs.

Behind him, Dora's cries pierced the silence of the graveyard. *How could a creature so small make such a big noise?*

The sky had lightened from dove grey to pale yellow. The parasol-pines towering above them were inky black.

As he stopped to catch his breath, Juba heard horse hooves pounding towards them. Their pursuers were about to catch sight of them.

He looked around desperately.

'There!' He pointed to the open doorway of a marble mausoleum, half hidden behind the trunks of dark umbrella pines up ahead. 'Let's hide in there! If we close the door maybe they won't hear her!'

But even as he led the way to the tomb, he knew it was hopeless.

Chapter Twelve
COLUMBARIUM

Ursula was running for her life and the life of her wailing baby sister. She stumbled after her brother, making for the white tomb.

But as she passed a row of red brick tombs, some with doors open and some with doors closed, a dark figure stepped in front of her.

Ursula squealed as she collided with a plump young woman in a black stola and palla.

The woman pulled Ursula into one of the tombs, grabbed the crying baby and put her under her palla. Instantly, Dora was silent.

Ursula stared in astonishment at the woman in black, and listened to the distinctive grunts of her baby sister feeding. Then she whirled as a figure blocked the bright doorway of the tomb. But it wasn't one of the soldiers or the hooded man; it was Fronto.

'I saw you go in here,' he gasped.

'Where's Juba?' Ursula cried.

'In the white tomb,' Fronto said. 'Where's Dora?'

Ursula pointed. 'Under her palla. She has milk!'

The woman looked up. 'Is someone chasing you?' she asked.

When Fronto nodded, the woman hissed, 'Then come in! And close the door!'

'Our brother is still out there,' Ursula cried. 'He went into the white tomb.'

'Bar the door,' the woman said to Ursula. 'Do you see the crack between the bottom of the door and the threshold? You might be able to see your brother from down there. When the coast is clear, tell this one to open it again.'

'All right!' Ursula's heart was racing like a rabbit's, but the silence of the tomb calmed her a little. She barred the door, then knelt down and tried to look out of the crack. She couldn't see anything at first but when she lay on her stomach and turned her head, her right eye could see the marble-faced mausoleum her brother had first gone for.

Above her, Fronto was whispering *right, left, right* over and over. She presumed he was touching the door frame.

Keeping her gaze fixed on the marble tomb, Ursula saw Juba's worried face appear in the doorway.

'Fronto!' she hissed, 'Lift the bar. No! Wait!'

She could hear hoof-beats and when she shifted the angle of her head a little she saw a blur of white horse legs. When the sound faded she stood up. 'Now!'

Fronto opened the door. Quick as a bolt of lightning, Ursula ran across the ground to the white tomb, grabbed her brother's hand and pulled him back to the smaller brick tomb.

'There was no door on that tomb,' he gasped, lowering the birdcage.

'There is on this one!' she cried, closing it and putting down the inner bar.

Once again, Ursula lay on her stomach and peered out of the

40

crack. She heard hoof beats but this time they were slower. Their pursuers were coming back.

She held her breath as they came closer and closer, and then passed by.

Ursula exhaled with relief and sat up.

'What happened to you?' Juba hissed. 'Where's the baby?'

'Shhh!' Ursula commanded. She pointed to the woman standing in the darkest corner of the lamplit tomb, nursing baby Dora.

'Praise the gods!' Juba whispered. 'Are you sure they've gone?'

For a third time, Ursula stretched out on her stomach and put her eye to the crack above the threshold.

At first she saw nothing, just part of the marble-faced tomb opposite, then she almost screamed as a man's hairy foot came into view. He was only a hands-breadth away, just the other side of the door.

Eyes wide, she turned to the others and put her finger to her lips.

They all held their breath.

Ursula put her ear to the crack just in time to hear a muffled voice.

'This one's locked,' said the voice.

'That one, too,' came a reply.

'They must have got past us. Let's go back to Ostia and search both harbours.' It was a man's voice: light, cultured and strangely familiar.

'Don't worry, sir,' said a second, deeper voice. 'We'll find them. And when we do, we'll make them pay.'

Chapter Thirteen
CINERARIA

In the dark tomb, Juba stared at the woman who had saved their lives.

'Who are you?' he asked. 'And how did you come to be here? It's like a miracle.'

'It's not *like* a miracle,' the woman said softly. 'It *is* a miracle.' She pointed at a glass jar in one of the niches in the wall.

Juba could see ashes and small bones through the blue-green glass. He gave an involuntary shudder.

'That is my baby girl,' the young woman said. 'She died yesterday. You probably saw the remains of her pyre outside. I was doing vigil and praying to my god. I was just about to go home when I heard you.'

Juba nodded. That explained why the woman had been in the graveyard at dawn. And why she had milk.

The woman pointed to another glass cremation urn. 'And that was my baby boy. And that. And that.'

Ursula gasped. 'You lost four babies?'

The woman nodded and even in dim lamplight Juba could see tears glitter in her dark eyes. 'They all sickened and died at six weeks.' The woman took Dora out from under her black palla and gazed into her face. 'How old is this beautiful girl?' she asked.

'Almost five months,' Ursula said.

'And who is chasing you?' The woman put Dora up against her shoulder and patted the baby's back.

'The Emperor's men,' Ursula said.

Juba frowned at her. If the woman knew they were wanted by the Emperor she might give them up to save herself, or for a reward.

Dora burped and the woman kissed her forehead. 'The Emperor's men?' she said.

Juba sighed. He could not take back Ursula's words, so he decided to tell the truth. 'Yes, it was soldiers from Domitian's Praetorian Guard,' he admitted. 'They broke into our house last night.'

The woman nodded. 'It is rumoured that Domitian has begun to seize the houses of the rich, and execute the owners. Are your parents . . .?' She looked at Fronto for confirmation, but he was busy touching all the urns on the shelves going from right to left so she turned to Juba.

Juba took a deep breath. 'Our parents stayed behind so we could escape.' He held her gaze for a long moment and when her eyes grew wide, he knew that she understood. 'They told us to go to Britannia,' he added.

'Britannia?' The woman looked puzzled. 'Why?'

'Our uncle lives there,' Ursula said.

'And it's far away from here,' Juba added.

'So you've come to Ostia hoping to board a ship sailing to Britannia?'

'Yes,' Juba said.

'How were you going to feed . . . What is her name?'

'We call her Dora,' Juba said, 'I am Lucius Domitius Juba. My sister is called Ursula and my older brother is Fronto.'

'My name is Calpurnia Firma,' said the woman. She looked at the baby, her eyes full of concern. 'How were you going to feed little Dora?'

'We were going to buy a slave girl to be a wet-nurse,' Juba said.

'Or maybe a goat,' Fronto said.

'But we were robbed,' Juba added.

'The Emperor's men robbed you?'

'No, some beggars in the graveyard outside Rome. My mother gave me a valuable gem to sell so I could pay for passage and maybe even a wet-nurse, but they took it along with all our money and good luck charms. Now we have nothing. Nothing but our household gods. And we can't sell those.'

Ursula clutched the woman's arm. 'Domina!' she cried. 'Could you come to Britannia with us to be our baby sister's wet nurse? We can't pay you now, but my uncle is very rich. He would pay you when you get there. Wouldn't he, Juba?'

Juba forced himself to smile. 'Yes!' he said. 'I know he would pay you. He would reward you very well.'

The woman shook her head. 'I'm sorry. I have a life here. I couldn't leave my husband and mother. But if you come home with me now, I will shelter you from the men pursuing you. We must protect this little one. My brother is a sailor,' she added. 'He might be able to find out about ships going to Britannia.' She looked at Ursula. 'Is it safe to come out yet? Have they gone?'

Ursula crouched down again and put first her eye, then her ear to the threshold crack. Finally, she nodded. 'I think so,' she said. 'They said they were going to the harbours.'

She cautiously opened the door of the tomb.

As they stepped out into bright morning light a voice said, '*What ARE you doing?*'

Ursula clapped her hands in delight. 'Loquax found us!' she cried, as her bird fluttered down to her shoulder.

'It's a good omen!' Fronto said.

But as they followed the woman through the tombs of Ostia's necropolis, Juba wondered if Loquax's cry had been a warning.

Chapter Fourteen
INSULA

Calpurnia Firma took Juba and his siblings to her ground floor home in a red brick apartment block near the Marina Harbour. Her living space had three sleeping cubicles. The smallest of these was a child's room. There were grey cupids painted on a deep red wall and just enough room for the three of them to lie on woven rush sleeping mats.

Wrapped in his cloak, Juba could feel something bumpy, about the size of a pebble. He tried to brush it away but it was too dark to see where it was.

Eventually he must have slept for when he opened his eyes, he could tell by the light coming through a small shuttered window that it was now late morning. The smell of fresh bread made his stomach growl. Leaving his woollen cloak on the mat, he got up and carefully stepped over Fronto, who was lying on his back with his mouth open. Ursula had been sleeping with her kitten but it was now exploring the folds of her cloak. He picked it up and closed the bedroom door softly behind him. Calpurnia Firma stood by a brick hearth in a spacious common room lit by two small windows and the open door. She was singing and stirring a small cauldron. A wicker baby's cradle hung from a kind of frame. He went over and looked in.

It was empty.

'Where's the baby?' Juba asked.

Calpurnia turned with a smile. 'In the courtyard with my mother. Mater likes to watch the comings-and-goings of our neighbours. Would you like some bread?'

'Yes, please,' Juba said. 'And something to drink.'

'The bread is almost ready,' she said and held out a copper beaker. 'Here is some posca. Give me the kitten. I'll feed her, too.'

Juba traded the kitten for a beaker of vinegar-tinted water and took a sip. Attracted by the sound of children playing and bright morning light, he went to the front door. Standing on the threshold, he could see a sunny inner courtyard through the pillars of a colonnade. It was a beautiful day: not too hot and with a fresh breeze. He stepped out onto the covered walkway and went to one of the columns. In the centre of the courtyard was a dusty fig tree with a goat tethered to its trunk. Seven or eight children were playing with a hoop at one end of the space. At the other end women were filling jars from a fountain and chatting happily. On one of the upper floors a woman had hung a carpet over the low wall of the walkway. She was beating the carpet with a wicker paddle and releasing clouds of dust, golden in the noon sunlight. When she saw him she waved cheerfully.

Juba was amazed to see how many people seemed to live in a space not much bigger than his parents' townhouse. And how happy they seemed.

When he turned to go back inside he saw a grey-haired woman in a wicker armchair, just outside Calpurnia's door. The old woman was holding baby Dora and watching him with bright black eyes. Loquax perched on the back of her chair.

'Hello,' Juba said politely. 'I'm Lucius Domitius Juba. That's my baby sister, Dora.'

The grey-haired woman did not reply, but her eyes smiled and she nodded.

Dora was sitting on the woman's lap, watching the children with intense interest. When she saw Juba she chortled and flapped her chubby arms at him. Then she turned her head to watch the children again. She was wearing little felt boots and an apricot-coloured tunic.

Juba went back inside.

Calpurnia was just putting a discus-shaped loaf of bread on the table. When she saw him she took his hands. He looked at her in surprise. In daylight he could see that she had smooth olive skin and dark glossy hair. Her brown eyes were full of compassion.

'Your parents are dead, aren't they?' she said softly.

Juba nodded. Then he hung his head and wept.

She did not say anything, or try to embrace him, but she kept hold of his hands. When he had regained control of himself she gave him a napkin to dry his tears. Then she led him to the table.

'Sit and eat. I have a proposal for you.'

Juba dutifully sat on a wooden bench. Calpurnia sat opposite him, broke the bread and gave him a piece. It was still warm from the oven, and delicious. As he ate, his spirits lifted a little.

When he finished his bread, Calpurnia handed him a red apple.

'How will you to get to Britannia?' she asked as he took a bite of the apple. 'Very few ships sail there directly. Do you know that most people go by land across Italia and Gaul and then take a ship from there? And whether by land or by sea, it is a thousand-mile journey. It will take you a month at least.'

Juba swallowed hard. The thought of taking his siblings a thousand miles made him feel dizzy.

'And do you have enough money for such a trip?'

He shook his head. 'The robbers took all our money. All we have left is a kitten, a talking bird, my brother's signet ring and the clothes we are wearing. Oh, and our household gods. But they are only valuable to us.'

Calpurnia nodded, her gaze intent. 'Then here is my proposal,' she said. 'My husband works for the guild of beast importers and my brother Quintus is a sailor. Between them they know every ship and sea captain in all three harbours. They will arrange for your passage by ship directly from here to Britannia. The voyage should only take about a month and the three of you will not have to pay a single quadrans. Not if you agree to the exchange.'

'What exchange?' Juba asked.

Calpurnia took a deep breath. 'Your sister Dora for your passage to Britannia.'

Juba almost choked.

'You want me to give you my baby sister?'

'It is the best solution for all of us,' she said. 'You will not be able to care for her. Even if you get her to Britannia, it is a cold and hostile country full of wolves and other wild beasts, not to mention the blue-painted barbarians. She would not survive long.'

'How do you know so much about Britannia?'

'My brother Quintus told me. He sailed there ten years ago. Leave Dora here with me. I will feed her and clothe her and sing to her. My husband is a kind man and a good provider. My mother cannot speak, but already she cherishes your baby sister. I promise,' vowed Calpurnia, 'that the three of us will love Dora to the tips of our fingers.'

'What about your husband?' Juba asked. 'Will he love her as his own? Will he want a baby with such dark skin?'

Calpurnia gave him a tearful smile. 'That is why this baby is a miracle,' she said. 'My husband Publius is from Sabratha. He has the darkest skin and the biggest heart of any man I have ever met.'

The hairs on Juba's arms and the back of his neck lifted.

It did seem like a miraculous answer to all their prayers.

And yet . . .

He remembered the moment his father had first taken him and his brother and sister into his mother's room to meet their newest sibling. How tiny baby Dora had seemed, nestled in his mother's arms. How his father's eyes had filled with tears of pride.

He remembered his mother's words: *Promise me you will do everything in your power to save the children.*

He took a deep breath and stared at the table.

I promised Mater I would protect them, he told himself. *But that was when we were rich. Now we have nothing. Dora is so little, so helpless. How will I feed her when she's hungry? Clothe her when she's wet? Pay for a doctor when she is unwell?*

How will she survive a thousand-mile journey by ship? How will I look after her in a strange land? This woman risked her life to help us and she really would look after Dora. She would feed her, love her, sing to her . . .

Juba dug his fingers into his scalp. *But if I leave Dora behind, my brother and sister will never forgive me. She is our own flesh and blood and we might never see her again.*

Dear Jupiter, he prayed. *Send me a sign. Show me what to do.*

Chapter Fifteen
CUPAE

For the second time in as many days, Fronto was woken in the middle of the night.

It was Calpurnia Firma.

'Soldiers are knocking on all the doors of the street,' she whispered. 'They're asking about three children and a baby. You must go now!'

Fronto nodded groggily. The lady's brother stood behind her. He had dark eyes and hair like his sister but was skinny as a spear. Her husband was in the main room. He was a big man with a brilliant smile. But he was not smiling now. Juba and Ursula stood ready, their cloaks fastened and hoods up.

As Fronto followed them into the dark courtyard, he tapped the door frame three times: *right, left, right.*

The lady from the tombs wasn't going to the docks with them, but she came out in her sleeping tunic and shawl, and kissed them each on the forehead. She gave Fronto a napkin with three honey cakes inside. He hurriedly stuffed them down the front of his cherry-red tunic.

In the courtyard he felt the damp night air and heard the cicadas chirping briskly. The dim light of the lamphorn showed Juba with a Dora-sized bump in the sling around his body and

Ursula with a kitten-sized bump in a much smaller sling. Fronto was given charge of Loquax in his covered cage.

Then Calpurnia Firma's big dark-skinned husband and her skinny brother led them through a maze of streets to the port. Unlike marble-clad Rome, Ostia was a town of red brick. And it smelled of the sea.

Fronto thought of all the things that could bring bad luck on a ship. You had to step off the gangplank onto the deck with your right foot, just like going into a house. You could not sneeze on board ship, or it would sink. You could not cut your hair or nails. It was bad luck if an owl or a black cat was on board. Ursula's kitten was grey, white and brown but what about a black bird like Loquax?

Finally they came out onto the docks. The wooden planks were springy under his boots; he could smell water and hear it slapping against the ships and the piers. They must be at the river harbour.

Now he began to make out the tall masts of ships. Flaming torches showed everything browny orange against the blackness. Warehouses with cartloads of amphorae outside. Big wooden crates on wheels with windows near the top. Straw for packing things and bales of hay for pack animals to eat. He thought he heard a lion roar and his stomach churned.

I'm not scared; I'm excited! It was something his father had taught him to say.

'Pollux!' cursed Calpurnia's brother. 'I see three men on white horses. Quickly! Inside this warehouse!'

Fronto felt himself shoved through a wide, dark doorway. A few hanging lamps showed barrels and small wooden crates. He could smell freshly cut wood. Sawdust prickled his nose and almost made him sneeze.

'By Jupiter!' cursed Calpurnia's husband, peeping out the door. 'They've dismounted and taken up a position where they can see all the ships. There's no way out!'

I'm not scared, Fronto told himself. *I'm excited.*

Then he had an idea.

He tugged the husband's tunic. 'The Trojan horse plan!' he whispered.

'What are you talking about?'

'The Greeks smuggled themselves into Troy inside a hollow wooden horse,' he explained. 'We can hide in hollow wooden barrels!'

The two men looked at each other, then grinned and nodded.

'I'm not scared; I'm excited,' Fronto murmured as they helped him get in a barrel. It was new and smelled of oak and fresh straw.

He put his arms round the birdcage and scrunched down. When they tapped a circular wooden lid in place, he was plunged into darkness.

'Hey!' he cried as he felt himself tip sideways, and now they were rolling him.

His stomach gurgled unhappily and he concentrated on trying not to crush the wicker cage with poor Loquax inside. He could hear cheeps of alarm.

'I'm not scared; I'm excited,' he whispered over and over.

He could feel them rolling him up the gangplank and wondered what kind of luck it brought if you did not use either foot to first step on the deck.

At last the barrel came to rest upright on a gently rocking surface and he knew he was safe.

As they prised open the lid and he saw their smiling faces he breathed a sigh of relief. They had done everything correctly.

They were on board the ship that would take them to Britannia.

It was only then that a thought occurred to him. Would he ever see home again?

II

Chapter Sixteen
NAVIS

Ursula had never felt so free as when she was lifted out of an oaken barrel onto the deck of the ship.

For almost her whole life, her parents had kept her safely indoors.

Even when they went to their country villa near Naples, she had to stay inside the carriage, lest a potential kidnapper spot her.

Her parents were nearly as rich as the Emperor but she had never been allowed a pet because they carried fleas, worms and other vermin, according to her mother.

She had only been taught to read and write basic words, because her father thought the best occupation for a Roman girl was weaving.

All day and every day she had been required to sit at the loom with her mother. She even had to weave in their Naples villa while her brothers went hunting or fishing.

Until now, trips to the flower market of Rome on festival days had been her biggest excitement.

So when they pulled the lid off her barrel and she heard a voice say 'Welcome aboard the *Centaur*, bound for Britannia,' she felt like a butterfly coming out of its wrapper.

Strong hands lifted her up and out and lowered her onto the wooden deck. Above her, a huge sail made of a hundred squares of linen cracked and flapped as the wind filled it. The upper half was golden in the light of the rising sun. Gulls soared behind them while half-naked men ran on deck or climbed the rigging.

They were under sail!

'Look, Meer!' she cried, pulling back part of the sling she had made for her kitten. 'We're at sea!'

Once more, strong hands gripped her. This time they lifted her to the ship's rail.

'Stay there, young domina. And hang on tight.' It was a leathery-skinned old man with blue eyes the same colour as his tunic.

Juba and Fronto were already there. Juba looked grim and Fronto seemed queasy. Her eldest brother was clinging to the rail with one hand and gripping Loquax's cage in the other.

'Is Loquax all right?' Ursula bent and pulled back a flap of the dark linen that covered his cage. Inside, Loquax fluffed his feathers in alarm. '*I'm not scared; I'm excited!*'

Ursula laughed. Making sure that Meer was secure, she held the polished rail and hopped up and down. 'I'm not scared, either!' she cried. 'I'm excited!'

Her brothers stared at her and some of the sailors laughed.

The ship was moving rapidly and they were already a stadium's length from land. In the dawn light, Ursula could see men on the docks rolling barrels or carrying amphorae. She could see mules pulling carts and sailors moving up and down the gangplanks of ships. Everyone on the docks was in motion.

Everyone except two soldiers in white-crested helmets and a man in a pointy-hooded brown cloak. They stood still as statues

58

on the dock, gazing towards the merchant ship *Centaur*, now under way. But Ursula didn't care: they were safe!

Putting up her hood, Ursula ran towards the front of the ship.

The deck rose and fell beneath her feet and she laughed in delight when the floor wasn't where she expected it to be. The wind pushed back her hood, ruffled her tight black curls and made her pine-green cloak flap like the wings of a bird.

Three times a fine spray of salt mist flew in her mouth and eyes, making her gasp in delight. It was like swimming, flying and running all mixed together.

When she was a few paces from the front of the ship, she held on to the polished oak rail and leaned out over the water. From here she could see an enormous eye painted on the side. The ship plunged and fine spray misted her face again. She ran to the other side and leaned far out and saw an eye there, too. The ship was like a living creature, dipping its nose in the water, then rising up for breath.

At the very front, where the prow made a V, was a short leaning-out mast with a sail lashed to it. Beyond it, six steps led up to a small platform where a lookout could stand. Nobody was there, so she boldly went up these steps. Water rushed below, like liquid blue-green glass.

She held onto the front rail and opened her mouth to suck in as much of the salty air as she could. The sky above was blue but the sea below was bluer. Further out, it was the same dark blue as one of her father's star sapphires.

'*Meeer?*'

A tiny paw emerged as Meer tried to climb out of her sling.

'I'd better not let you out up here,' Ursula laughed. 'You might blow away!'

The steps leading back down to the deck were wet with sea spray, so she went down carefully. Underneath the lookout platform was a wedge-shaped space with coiled ropes and wooden buckets. It was sheltered from the wind and spray. She crawled into the shelter of this cubbyhole and carefully extracted the kitten from the small sling. She had to be careful because Meer's tiny claws kept catching on the fabric.

Meer tried to use her claws to grip the smooth planks of the deck, but the oak was silky smooth.

Mewing, the kitten would walk a few steps, then slide until she reached one of the worm-sized ridges of black pine pitch between the oaken planks.

'*Meeer!*'

Ursula clapped her hands in delight.

Suddenly the boat tipped and the tiny kitten tumbled past the place where the small mast came out of the deck. Ursula realised that there were long holes in the side of the boat at deck level, presumably to let seawater flow out after big waves crashed onto it. And now her kitten was sliding straight for one of these holes.

Chapter Seventeen
BRASSICA

Juba was watching the two soldiers and the mysterious hooded man on the pier when he heard his sister scream. He whirled, his heart in his throat.

Ursula was kneeling at the front of the ship by the bowsprit. A sailor in a long nutmeg-coloured tunic was standing over her.

'What's that sailor doing to Ursula?' Juba muttered, half to his brother and half to himself. 'He's made her cry!'

Anger rose up in him like hot vinegar added to soda.

He had paid a huge price for their passage on this ship.

Muttering a curse, Juba strode across the deck. Fronto grabbed Loquax's cage and followed.

'Who are you?' Juba demanded of the young sailor, who was now crouching in front of Ursula. 'And what are you doing to my sister?'

'*What ARE you doing?*' Loquax said from his cage.

The sailor looked round.

He was about Fronto's age and very good-looking, with dark hair and grey eyes.

'Are you addressing me?' the youth demanded in a cultured accent.

Juba felt his anger grow hotter. Was the sailor mocking him?

'Yes, I'm addressing you!' Juba clenched his fists. 'I asked what you were doing to my sister.'

'He wasn't doing anything to me!' Ursula scrambled to her feet. 'Meer almost got washed overboard and he saved her life. See?' She held out the sodden and shivering kitten, which looked smaller than ever.

'Your sister is correct,' said the sailor. 'I was merely saving her pet.'

'Oh.' Juba's anger started to drain away. The boy's cultured accent seemed genuine. Juba observed that his skin was as pale as a girl's and his long tunic made of fine linen. This boy was not a sailor; he was a passenger.

'May I ask what you are doing on this ship?' Juba said coldly. 'I chartered it at great expense. I was told that we would be the only passengers.'

The boy raised a dark eyebrow and stood up. He was taller than Juba by about two fingers. 'I'm not a passenger,' he said in an equally cool tone. 'My name is Castor and I am the owner of this ship.'

'The owner?' Juba stared in disbelief. The boy could not be much older than he was.

'Yes,' Castor said. 'And I risked the Emperor's anger by agreeing to take the three of you on board. And as for the price you paid,' he added with a sneer, 'I'm surprised you can sleep at night.'

'What does he mean?' Ursula said. 'What price did we pay?'

'You haven't told them, have you?' Castor folded his arms and looked down his nose at Juba.

'Told us what?' Fronto asked, looking from one to the other.

Juba hung his head. 'I didn't have a choice,' he muttered. 'She's better off this way.'

'Because we left in such a hurry,' said Castor, 'we are three sailors short. You may have paid a terrible price for your passage but if you want to eat you'll have to work for it.'

'What? All three of us?'

'Yes, all three of you. Otherwise I'll have to punish you.'

'You can't do that!' cried Juba.

'Oh, but I can,' said Castor with a faint smile. 'We'll be stopping at a dozen ports on our way. I can put you off at any one of them. You're on my ship now.'

Holding on to the rail, he made his way to the little cabin behind the mainsail.

'Juba!' Ursula cried. 'Why were you so mean to that boy? He saved my kitten! And he was being nice to me. He asked if I minded helping the crew and when I said no, he promised to let us share his cabin at night.'

Juba stared at the deck and shook his head. 'How was I to know he was the owner? It looked like he was bullying you.'

Fronto was frowning. 'Can we still sleep in the cabin?'

'I don't think so.' Juba glared at the small structure near the ship's mast. 'We'll have to sleep on deck with the crew.'

Ursula frowned, too. 'Juba, what did he mean by the price of the passage to Britannia?'

Juba shook his head.

'You said Uncle Pantera was going to send gold to Calpurnia and her family,' Fronto said.

'I lied,' Juba admitted.

Ursula looked puzzled. 'You're still wearing your clothes and you didn't have anything else left to give them . . .' Her voice trailed off and Juba saw her face darken.

'Juba, you didn't!'

'I had no choice,' he said, swallowing hard. 'Dora would

never have survived the sea voyage. Thirty days or more? How would we even feed her?'

'There's a goat in a cage behind the cabin,' said Ursula. 'We could have used her milk.'

Fronto frowned at Juba. 'Are you saying you traded Dora?'

Ursula nodded. 'That's exactly what he's saying! She was the price of our passage. So what's in here?' She pulled back the flap of Juba's cloak to reveal the lumpy sling. She reached in angrily and pulled out a cabbage and a big loaf of bread.

'Dora was never there!' Ursula cried, throwing down the cabbage. 'You tricked us!'

'Ursula, Fronto,' Juba said. 'Listen: Calpurnia vowed that she and her mother and her husband will love Dora to the tips of their fingers. Our sister will have a good life.'

'You don't know that!' cried Ursula. 'What if they have an unlucky life? What if the lady dies and the husband sells Dora as a slave? A thousand things could go wrong! But the worst of it is you didn't even ask us.'

'You would have taken her with you!' he cried. 'Like every stray kitten or injured bird you come across.'

'Dora is not a kitten or bird!' Ursula shouted back. 'She was our baby sister.'

'Thank the gods!' he cried. 'Your kitten was almost washed overboard and your bird keeps flying off. I promised I'd look after you all. I thought it was the best way to protect Dora.'

'What happens when Mater and Pater come to us in Britannia?' Ursula demanded. 'What will you tell them?'

Juba turned away. He didn't want them to see his face.

If they did, they might guess the truth.

Chapter Eighteen
VIRGA

Next day the arrogant young owner of the merchant ship *Centaur* watched as the captain gave Juba and his siblings their tasks for the next few weeks.

Arms folded, Castor stood in the door of his cabin, slightly above the rest of them. Juba wondered how he had ever taken the youth for a sailor. He wore a long tunic of nutmeg-coloured linen whereas the other three crew members wore only loincloths. Juba got the impression that they might have worn nothing at all had Ursula not been on board.

White-haired Captain Caerulus was the only other man wearing a tunic. It was short and sky blue.

Watched by Castor, the captain gave Fronto the job of polishing all the brass fittings and also helping the sailors weigh anchor and pull ropes.

When he turned to Ursula, she stuck her tongue out at him and scampered up the rope ladder on the mast until she was as high as she could go.

The captain shaded his eyes. 'You've just chosen your job, little girl!' he shouted up at her. 'You can be lookout and stay up there from dawn till dusk, except for meals.' He glanced back at Castor who gave him an almost imperceptible nod.

Finally, Captain Caerulus turned to Juba. 'See this stone?' he asked, holding out something that looked like a fat discus of bread. 'I want you to use it to polish the deck of the ship every morning. When you've finished that, you can be a general dogsbody to the others. That means you do whatever they tell you to do from emptying the master's chamberpot to gutting fish.'

Juba stared in cold fury at the strange bread stone. He made no move to take it.

Captain Caerulus strode forward, and stopped with his tunic almost touching Juba's nose and the stone pressing Juba's chest.

Juba took the stone.

'Get down on your hands and knees!' said the Captain in a loud voice, 'I'll tell you how it's done.' Then he added in a low growl, 'Best do as I say, lad, and not make trouble. The young master's in a bad temper.'

Juba felt the eyes of the other three crew members on him. He took a quick step to the side so that the Captain did not block his view of Castor. 'I will not get down on my hands and knees to any man!' he cried. 'I'm not your slave!' With that, he hurled the stone at the ship's young owner.

Castor's mouth was an O as the stone hit the frame of the door a hands-breadth from his head and thudded back onto the deck. His handsome face went very pale.

He turned to the Captain. 'Use the switch,' he commanded. 'A dozen strokes.' And to Juba, 'I don't care who you traded for your passage to Britannia. While you are on my ship you follow my rules.' He retreated into his cabin and shut the door.

Juba felt two sailors grasp his arms. Another stepped forward to fumble at his cloak toggle.

'I'll do it!' he snapped. But his hands trembled as he took off his father's cloak and swayed on the moving deck of the ship.

'Best take off your tunic, too,' growled the Captain. 'Skin will heal. Wool has to be mended.'

Juba took out the figure of the god Mercury, who helped travellers on their way, and handed it to Fronto. He undid his belt, removed it, then pulled the tunic over his head and threw it on the deck.

The sea breeze made his skin like gooseflesh and he shivered. He wanted to shout *You can't do this!*

But he knew they *could*.

He was at their mercy; he had no rights on board the *Centaur*.

'Hang on to the mast and don't let go,' said Captain Caerulus, taking a slender birch rod from his belt. 'Or we'll have to bind your hands while we do it.'

Juba relectantly hugged the mast. The wood was cold against the naked skin of his chest. The posture was humiliating. He had beaten his own slave once or twice. His father had shown him how to take a birch rod and flick it smartly across the boy's back.

In a strange way he almost felt that he deserved it. He had given away his baby sister to save the rest of them.

Besides, how bad could it be? It wasn't a leather strap studded with nails and knots. It was just a birch rod like one he had used.

The first blow stung like a giant wasp and he heard himself yelp. Hot shame flooded his face.

He clenched his jaw and promised himself he would not cry out again. He would be brave, like Aeneas. He thought of the four pillars of Stoicism that his father had taught him: Justice, Moderation, Courage and Wisdom.

Right now, he needed Courage.

A saying often quoted by his father came into his head: *Courage is being ready for any emergency.*

When the Captain finally stepped back and said, 'That's all, lad,' Juba took a moment to compose his face. Then he unwrapped his arms from the mast and moved stiffly away. He tried to walk steadily to the rail, but it was hard with the ship moving under his feet.

What hurt more than his back was knowing he had once done this to his own slave.

Two of the crew members busied themselves with their own tasks and avoided looking at him but the third – a sailor with bright blue eyes and blond hair cropped short – brought a basin with vinegar-tinted water and a sea-sponge in it. He set it on the deck at Juba's feet and went quietly away. Fronto was there and he gently used the sponge to bathe the welts.

Juba gritted his teeth and grunted his thanks.

Only one of the blows had broken the skin. It was on his waist, under his lowest right rib. When the vinegar touched it he had to bite his lip to stop from crying out.

When his brother had finished bathing the wounds on his back, Juba eased on his tunic and cinched his belt lower than usual. He dropped the Mercury statue back in, and its weight comforted him a little.

As he turned to make his way to the back of the ship, something fell with a thunk at his feet. It was the bread stone. Captain Caerulus stood nearby with his arms folded and his white eyebrows raised.

Juba took a deep breath and tried not be sick. *Courage!* he told himself. And to Captain Caerulus he said, 'Show me how to do it?'

The Captain nodded and gave him a small wink.

'Good lad,' he said.

Chapter Nineteen
OCEANUS

Captain Caerulus took Juba to the front of the ship and showed him how to polish the deck with his disk of pumice. Using circular motions he had to rub the oak planks, working backwards as he went. Afterwards he sluiced the boards with buckets of seawater. When the sun dried them they were a milky buff colour and smooth as silk.

Over the following weeks, he got faster until he was able to complete it in one hour. It was exhausting work. As soon as he finished he had to do whatever the sailors wanted, usually the worst jobs: emptying the latrine bucket, helping bring amphorae up from the dank hold, or taking night watch.

Food was a luxury and they were allowed just two bowls of millet porridge a day plus a ration of hard ship's biscuit. But they could only have their dinner if they asked for it in Brittonic. Castor was learning the language of the Britons and threatened to use the cane on anyone who spoke Latin.

As the three sailors were from Britain and Captain Caerulus had served there for many years, this threat only applied to Juba and his siblings.

Juba and Fronto tried their best to comply, but Ursula resisted.

Already furious at Juba for leaving baby Dora behind, she refused to ask for her evening bowl of porridge in Brittonic even though Nantonius the cook kept whispering the phrase.

When Castor told Nantonius not to fill her bowl, she glared defiantly at him and then clambered up the rope ladder to the lookout's basket.

She stayed there all night, sharing the skin of goats' milk that Calpurnia had filled for Meer.

Next day he heard her exchanging a few words of Brittonic with the youngest sailor, Bubo, when they were up in the rigging together.

And on the third day she asked for porridge in a low voice, but with perfect pronunciation.

Every afternoon, when the *Centaur* came into a new port, the sailors would unload amphorae of wine and bring back the specialty of the region. From Antipolis they brought jugs of fish-sauce, from Forum Julii hemp bags full of freshly cut lavender and from Massilia sheets of curved cork.

A week out of Ostia, the welts on Juba's back had healed and the blisters on his hands had become callouses. Two weeks out, he realised he was becoming stronger. At the beginning of the voyage, he had barely been able to roll one of the big amphorae. Now he could lift one easily, and Fronto could lift two.

By the time they reached the port of Baelo Claudia in the province of Baetica, he and Fronto had begun to help the sailors load and unload. At night he and his brother and sister diced with the crew, listened to their stories and gnawed ship's biscuit. Juba's Brittonic was becoming fluent, his body was stronger than it had ever been and his dreams were scented with lavender.

He was almost content.

Then, three weeks out, they passed through the Pillars of Hercules and everything changed.

They were now on Oceanus, where the water was a deep blue, almost black in places. And it was choppier. The wind was different, too. It was cold and whined constantly in his ears. Sea spray made the ropes slippery and harder to pull. The worst part of the day was first thing, when he had to scrub the deck in freezing spray while the boat bucked and twisted like a wild horse.

The bitter wind soured the mood of the sailors. It even affected Loquax. For the first time, the bird fell silent and the sailors stopped coming to leave titbits in his cage. The fragrant lavender went down into the hold, so that it would not become sodden.

Castor had always kept aloof, taking aside one of the three British sailors to speak with for hours at a time. At first he did this at the front of the ship, but with the sea change he spent most of the day in his cabin. Whenever they passed they could hear him speaking Brittonic with whichever sailor was teaching him that day.

One night, huddled together on the hard, damp deck and shivering in the chilly night air, Juba could hear Ursula's teeth chattering.

'I hate Castor!' she muttered. 'He's warm and dry in his cabin while we have to freeze out here.'

'It's my fault,' Juba said. 'If I hadn't lost my temper . . .'

Ursula didn't reply. She still hadn't forgiven him for selling their baby sister.

Instead she turned to Fronto.

'I have an idea,' she said. 'I'm going to pretend to be nice. That way I can find out about him.'

'Why would you do that?' Fronto asked her.

'To get the best revenge,' she said.

Chapter Twenty
PANIS NAUTICUS

Next morning a choppy sea and northerly breeze kept them busy until midday, when a lessening of the wind allowed them to gnaw their ration of ship's biscuit. Ursula was sitting with her back against the ship's rail by a small wooden shrine in the stern of the boat.

She was in her usual place with Fronto between her and Juba so she didn't have to look at him. But now their plot to punish Castor made it necessary for them to work together. Although she would never forgive Juba for selling their sister, it was a relief to be able to speak to him again.

They had been discussing their plot when the Captain interrupted them.

'You should kiss Castor's feet!' He was speaking Latin rather than Brittonic.

'What do you mean?' Ursula had been sucking her piece of ship's biscuit to make it soft. She looked at the Captain.

'I mean you should kiss his feet in gratitude.'

'Why should we be grateful to him?' Juba glowered.

The Captain kept one hand on the tiller and turned round. 'Because when the three of you first arrived I thought you'd be goners.'

'What do you mean?' Fronto asked.

'I mean you were plump, pampered and posh. If he'd let you hide out in his cabin reading scrolls, you'd be in no shape to survive in Britannia.'

Ursula scowled at him. 'Why not? Because it's a cold and hostile country full of wolves and other wild beasts?' She lifted her chin. 'I like animals.'

Captain Caerulus frowned. 'It's not just the animals. The Britons are the most savage race you will find. Their warriors run around naked, covered in blue tattoos. They put clay in their hair, which they wear long. When it dries they look like the sun god with their hair all sticking out in spiky rays. And when they kill you – and they will kill you, be sure of that – they cut off your head and keep it so your spirit can't go down to the underworld.'

Ursula refused to let him frighten her. 'So why should we be grateful?' she asked, working at the ship's biscuit with her back teeth.

'Because now you have half a chance of surviving. You're used to hard tack, hard work and sleeping on a hard deck. You've developed good arm muscles for climbing trees and good leg muscles for running away.'

'I've heard the women fight, too,' Fronto said.

'Indeed they do!' said the Captain. 'When I was in the army I fought a tribe led by a woman.'

Ursula leaned forward. 'A woman led an army?'

'Boudica her name was.' A faraway look came into the Captain's blue eyes, as if he were recalling an old girlfriend. 'She was queen of a northern tribe. She was a great leader: six foot tall with brass-coloured hair down to her hips. She could throw a spear and drive a chariot.'

'I think I've heard of her,' Juba said. 'Is she the one who drove a chariot with curved blades coming out of the wheels?'

Captain Caerulus snorted. 'That's a myth. If you put blades on your wheels you'd chop your own men to bits.'

Fronto cocked his head. 'Does she run around naked, covered in blue tattoos and with her long hair spiked out?'

Captain Caerulus laughed. 'First, she's dead these past thirty or so years. Second, she did not go naked. She wore a long tunic with lots of criss-crossing coloured stripes. Around her neck she had a twisty gold necklace as thick as your sister's wrist.'

'Our father showed us something like that once,' said Juba. 'He called it a torc.'

'That's right. Boudica wore a solid gold torc.'

'She sounds wonderful,' said Ursula.

But Juba shook his head. 'She sounds terrifying.'

'*I'm not scared*,' Loquax chimed in. '*I'm excited.*'

Ursula and her brothers laughed but the Captain remained grave. 'She *was* terrifying,' he said. 'I was lucky to get out alive. The things she did to her captives . . . Well, it's too horrible to say.'

'If Boudica is dead,' Ursula said. 'What do we have to be afraid of?'

'Why, all them other savage tribes,' said Captain Caerulus. 'And if they don't get you, the weather will. But like I said, you have a better chance of surviving now than you did when you came on board. That's why you should kiss the young master's feet.'

Chapter Twenty-One
MATELLA

Several times a day – when he was not speaking with the sailors – Castor sat at the front of the ship gazing pensively at the horizon. Perhaps he was praying to his god. Maybe he was remembering the past or imagining the future. Ursula did not know and she did not care. All she wanted was revenge.

The sky above was ominous, with clouds the colour of an angry bruise. But Castor was alone at the front and this was her best chance to distract him. She went up quietly on her bare feet and leaned against the rail.

'The Captain said we should thank you,' she said.

She pretended not to look at him, but out of the corner of her eye she saw his expression change.

'Why?' He frowned.

'He says our month aboard the *Centaur* has made us ready to live in Britannia. He says we've changed a lot.'

'You have changed a lot,' Castor admitted. 'Not you so much, but your brothers.'

His words stung. 'What do you mean, *not me so much*?'

He turned to face her. She had not been this close to him since the first day when he had saved her kitten. His pale skin made him look younger and somehow vulnerable.

'Your brothers have to muster their courage,' he said. 'You are naturally brave.'

She looked at him in astonishment. He was complimenting her!

Then he said something even more surprising.

'You mustn't be hard on Juba.'

She stared. He was telling her to be nice to her brother even as they were putting the finishing touches on their revenge.

Castor gazed at the horizon. 'When I heard he gave up your baby sister in return for your passage to Britannia I was furious.'

'Me too!' Ursula said.

Castor nodded. 'But now I think he made the right decision. I was angry with him because I lost my brother when I was little.'

'You did?'

'Yes. My father and mother, too.'

He turned his head to look at her. His eyes were grey. Not the greenish grey of her brothers but a stormy blue-grey, like the sky above. He slowly reached towards her and for a moment she thought he was going to stroke her cheek. Instead he began to pet Meer, perched on her shoulder. The kitten began to purr.

'It's a long story,' he said. 'Maybe one day I'll tell you.'

Ursula swallowed hard.

As much as she had hated Castor before, her heart melted for him.

A few spots of rain stung her face.

Castor stood up. 'It looks like a storm is coming,' he said. 'I'd better go inside. Do you want to come, too? Captain Caerulus is right; I was only hard on you for your own interest. But you're strong enough now.'

Ursula stared at him. He had to pick this very moment to

invite her into his cabin? The moment when his own chamberpot full of urine was balanced on the half open door, ready to fall and drench him?

She knew what she had to do. 'Yes,' she said. 'I would love to shelter with you.' And before he could protest, she handed him Meer and ran for the door of his cabin, knowing she would suffer the punishment that she had chosen for him.

Chapter Twenty-Two
DUBRIS

In a way, the terrible storm that followed was good for each of them.

It was good for Ursula because it prevented Castor from punishing her for their cruel prank, which she now regretted to the core of her being. Before he had been able to say anything she had scrambled up into the lookout's basket and strapped herself to the mast. Then the storm was upon them.

If the mast went, she would go with it. Days dissolved into nights as she kept watch for signs of rocks or sandbars that could finish them. The stinging sheets of rain and flying packets of saltwater scrubbed all the urine from her skin and cloak and hair. She was miserable because she had left Meer with Castor and did not know if her kitten was dead or alive. Three times during the storm Bubo managed to climb up to give her a sodden chunk of ship's biscuit, which was the only food they could eat. But the swaying of the mast was so violent that she could barely keep it down.

The storm was good for Fronto because it showed him how strong he had become. A month earlier he would have taken shelter in the goat's cage and tapped obsessively on the narrow doorway. Now he was too busy helping the sailors keep the sails lashed tight and making sure the ship had her nose to the swells. In Rome he had been used to sleeping for ten hours a night and had enjoyed up to five meals a day. On board *Centaur* he went for two nights with no sleep and three days with no food. At one point, when they were attaching another forestay to the mainmast, a violent lurch almost shook him from the rigging. He was holding on to a twist of rope with one hand. The rest of his body was swinging free, flying in the salty sweet spray of rain mixed with wave. But instead of fear, he felt a strange wild joy. He felt like a god, flying in a world of grey-green sea foam.

The roar of the storm receded and a voice in his head said very clearly, *It is not your time.* And sure enough, Nantonius had grasped his wrist and wrenched him back onto the yardarm with superhuman strength.

The storm was good for Juba because it convinced him that his decision to leave Dora behind had been right. On the first day of the storm the goat was washed overboard, cage and all. On the second night a wave destroyed Castor's cabin and he only survived because Captain Caerulus caught his ankle as a wave tumbled him past.

On the third morning the storm finally abated. Juba fell asleep on the sodden deck after uttering a heartfelt prayer, 'Thank you, Jupiter, Mercury and Venus, that I didn't bring Dora with us. I don't know how she would have survived.'

Exhausted, they lay on the deck, their clothes steaming in the bright autumn sunshine, while red-eyed Captain Caerulus stood lashed to the steering oar, waiting until one of them should take his place. Eventually Castor stood and let the Captain sleep while he kept the ship's prow pointing towards a streak of white on the horizon that might be the cliffs of Dubris.

At first they thought Meer the kitten had perished along with the goat, but she emerged from the hold on the fourth day, so skinny that she could hardly walk. There was no milk for her, so she ate salt beef pre-chewed by Ursula. It was the first solid food she had tasted.

Loquax's cage had been hung in the hold and he was so miserable after three days without food that he would not speak or fly. But they were all alive.

And Britannia, the province at the edge of the world, was finally in sight.

Chapter Twenty-Three
RUTUPIAE

They reached Britannia later that afternoon. The crew raised a tired cheer as the band of white on the horizon became the cliffs of Dubris, with a thousand seagulls circling overhead. Late in the afternoon, they dropped anchor at Rutupiae, the port from which Emperor Claudius had launched his invasion of the island fifty years before.

Everyone but Castor went ashore. Each of them cut a lock of hair and dedicated it at the temple of Neptune in thanks for a safe landfall. They admired the huge triumphal arch with elephants on top. That night Captain Caerulus took them all to have dinner at a harbour side inn and they feasted on oysters and beans. Most of the next day was spent repairing damage to the *Centaur* and buying fresh provisions.

They left Rutupiae on the third day after the storm.

On the morning of the fourth – the Nones of October – an easterly breeze brought them into a great estuary under a milky sky with marsh birds rising and settling around them. Soon the wind died, but a tide carried them on. The trees on the distant banks were bluish green rather than the golden green of Italian trees.

'*Aeneas looks over the surface of the deep and sees a great forest,*' quoted Fronto from the rigging. '*He tells his comrades to bend their prows towards land and is happy to enter the shaded river.*'

'If I can find the blasted river,' muttered Captain Caerulus. 'The mouth of the Thamesis is a beast to navigate.'

'I see a ship up ahead going the same direction as we are,' called Ursula from the highest part of the mainmast. 'It's much bigger than ours and has a red painted goose at the stern.'

'We'll follow it!' cried Captain Caerulus. 'Praise Neptune.'

Juba looked up from scouring the deck. The sun god Helios was high in the sky, covered by a thin veil of cloud, which dulled his light.

Gradually the wooded banks drew closer on either side and they could hear birdsong. Some of the trees were already losing their leaves; others were turning brown, orange and even red. Then came the first signs of civilisation: men digging pits on the banks for clay, sand and gravel. Round huts with thatched roofs gave way to plaster-covered buildings and even a few brick ones. Boats appeared on the river up ahead: merchant ships like theirs, but also flat barges and round coracles of wicker and hide.

They had just finished their duties when they passed the merchant ship with the red goose-head. She had dropped anchor in the deepest part of the river and her crew were transferring amphorae and sacks to a flotilla of small barges.

'It's low tide.' The captain pushed the steering oar to give her a wide berth. 'I suppose her draft is too deep for this river, but we should be fine. We're only little.'

The first wooden wharves had come into sight, so they hurried to the other side of the *Centaur* to look.

In his usual place at the prow of the ship, Castor stood with his black woollen cloak billowing out behind him. He had not spoken one word to Juba and the others since the storm.

At the stern, Captain Caerulus steered them closer to the north bank.

The wharves were similar to Ostia's, and so were the people walking on them. Some of the men had fair hair and moustaches. But most looked Roman, and some had skin the colour of his, or even darker.

'They don't look that different,' murmured Juba.

'Where are the naked, blue-tattooed people?' Fronto was craning his neck.

'I don't see any,' Ursula said. 'But look at that man with the two giant dogs. They're almost as big as ponies!'

'Is this Londinium?' Juba asked Captain Caerulus.

'It is indeed,' said the captain.

Four small boats rowed up to them. 'Festival today!' called one of the men in heavily accented Latin. 'Warehouses mostly closing for so people can attend the games.'

When Castor heard this he went to confer with Captain Caerulus. Then, without a word to Juba or the others, he climbed down a rope ladder into one of the boats.

'Where's he gone?' Juba asked the Captain as he watched Castor drift away. Castor had his hood up and his back to them as the man rowed him towards the wharves.

'On his quest, whatever that may be,' Captain Caerulus said, shaking his head. 'I've orders to catch the outgoing tide so we can deliver the rest of our wine to Camulodunum.'

'Are there camels at Camulodunum?' Ursula asked.

'No, just a lot of thirsty men,' the captain replied. 'And unless you want to meet them, I suggest you get into one of these other boats.'

'What?' cried Fronto. 'Go down that rope ladder?'

'What fun!' cried Ursula. 'Come on, Meer! Hang on tight. Juba, hand me Loquax once I'm in.'

Juba nodded and helped first Ursula and then Fronto descend the rope ladder into a small boat with a greasy-haired boatman. Nantonius brought a boathook and Juba lowered Loquax in his covered cage.

Juba looked around the ship for the last time. The *Centaur* had been their home for over a month and he realised he would miss it. He was about to swing his leg over the rail when Captain Caerulus put a meaty hand on his shoulder.

'It's hard being captain,' he said in a low voice. 'Sometimes you have to make hard decisions. But you did good. Keep doing the best for your crew.' He nodded down at Ursula and Fronto.

The Captain's firm touch and words of encouragement brought a sudden flood of emotion to Juba's heart. Tears sprang to his eyes and he turned away so the Captain would not think less of him.

'See that building?' Captain Caerulus pointed towards the docks with a stubby finger. 'That is the customs house. Ask the official about your uncle there. If Pantera is as famous as you say, then he will know where to find him.'

Juba nodded and took a breath. 'Thank you,' he said, trying to keep his voice steady. 'Thank you for everything.'

Caerulus pressed two coins into Juba's hand.

'Here,' he said. 'The young master told me to give you these. You worked as hard as any of us. The gold is wages for the three of you and the brass is for the boatman.'

Juba's eyes widened when he saw the two coins. The dupondius was worth half a sestertius. The aureus was worth one hundred.

'Will you thank Castor?' Juba asked.

'I might not see him again for a time,' said the Captain. 'I'm to be here on the full moon of next month. If he's not back, I'm to return to Ostia for the winter. It will be another half a year before the *Centaur* returns, gods permitting.' He made the sign against evil.

'Juba!' Fronto called from boat below. 'Come on! I'm hungry! I want a honey cake.'

Captain Caerulus chuckled and slapped Juba on the back. 'Good luck and farewell.'

'*Vale*,' Juba replied. He went down the rope ladder carefully; it was harder than it looked.

'What did the Captain give you?' Ursula asked Juba, as the boat pulled away from the *Centaur*.

Juba leaned forward so the boatman could not hear. 'An aureus,' he whispered. 'It's from Castor.'

'I wish I could have said goodbye to him,' said Ursula with a wistful sigh.

Fronto nodded his agreement but did not speak. Since the storm his brother had found a new sense of calm.

Juba looked for Castor on the docks but saw no sign of him. So he turned to watch the two rowing boats pull the *Centaur* round to face downstream.

A breeze ruffled the browny-grey surface of the Thamesis and Captain Caerulus bellowed out a command. Two of the crewmen scrambled up into the rigging and the familiar sail unfurled. Juba's home for the past six weeks was sailing back towards the estuary.

The *Centaur* was well on its way when their skiff bumped up against the timber wall that formed the side of the wharf.

The greasy-haired boatman threw a rope to a waiting boy who moored the boat. Juba was first up the damp wooden ladder to the wooden quayside. He took Loquax in his cage from Ursula and then helped her up.

Most of the warehouses were closing, or closed. Juba watched one man place shutter boards in the open front of a shop, step out through a narrow night door, then pull it shut and lock it.

Fronto was the last up the ladder and as he put his right foot down on the dock, a watery sun came out.

'It's a good omen!' cried Fronto.

Juba hoped he was right. He pointed towards a plaster and timber building with a clay tile roof. 'The Captain said someone at the customs house might know where Uncle Pantera lives. But we can't let them know he's our uncle, in case the Emperor's men are still after us. Let me do the talking.'

Chapter Twenty-Four
LONDINIUM

As Juba led his brother and sister towards the customs house, seagulls circled overhead, complaining and chuckling. Under his feet, the wet wooden wharf steamed in the autumn sunshine. The planks felt strangely solid after six weeks on the constantly moving surface of the *Centaur*'s deck. On his right were shut-up wooden warehouses, on his left the boats.

If Rome is marble and Ostia is brick, thought Juba, *then Londinium is wood.*

Even the customs house was wood beneath its coat of plaster.

A line of people stood outside, waiting to pass through.

'Is this for the customs official?' Juba asked the man at the end.

The man turned and looked down at him. He had slanting black eyes and a little black beard and brown skin. 'Yes, most certainly,' he said in accented Latin.

A distant roar came from the northwest.

'What was that?' asked Fronto.

'It sounded like people cheering,' said Ursula.

'Games in the amphitheatre,' said the man with the beard. 'Today is a festival. Everything closed at midday.' He gestured at the shuttered warehouses. Then he cocked his head. 'Where are you from?'

Juba hesitated. 'Ostia. We've come from Ostia.'

'Do you have somewhere to stay?'

Juba nodded. 'I hope so,' he said.

The bearded man smiled. 'If you need lodgings in Londinium, my brother recently opened a hospitium called the Phoenix. He says there is a fortune to be made in this fast-growing town. My name is Pygmalion,' he added. 'I'm from Phoenicia. And are you from one of the African provinces, too?'

Juba was wondering how much he should tell the man when a familiar voice cried, '*What ARE you doing?*'

Juba whirled just in time to see a grubby boy with reddish hair running away. He darted behind some barrels.

Juba frowned. 'What was that about?'

'Probably a cutpurse,' said Pygmalion.

Juba's heart jumped into his throat and he fumbled in his belt pouch for the gold coin.

'Thank the gods,' he breathed. 'It's still here.'

'Thank that bird,' said the man. 'You must be always alert. My brother told me crooks in Londinium are as thick as fleas on a camel. That's why I wear this.' He showed Juba a bracelet round his left wrist. It looked like a leather pouch but was made of bronze. He rattled it. 'My coins and jewels are in the hollow part,' he said. 'But you can't get at them unless you take the bracelet off first by means of this clasp. I see you are travelling light, too. Have you brought jewels as I did?'

'No,' said Juba. 'Only enough gold to get us to where we're going. I hope.'

Pygmalion grinned. 'Did you hear the joke about the philosopher at the customs house? The tax collector asks him what he has to declare and he says "Only Prudence, Chastity and Honour!" And the tax collector says, "Three slave-girls, eh? You'll have to pay tax on those!" Get it?' The Phoenician laughed heartily at his own joke and slapped his thigh.

When they entered the customs house, Juba saw a dark-haired man sitting at a desk covered with scrolls and wooden tablets. On one side of the room was a clerk with weights, measures and coins. Two soldiers stood behind him.

'Names?' The man regarded them with sleepy eyes.

Juba gave him made-up names.

The man made a note on a wax-tablet. 'Anything to declare?' he said, without looking up.

Juba opened his hands. 'Only the clothes we're wearing and my sister's pets.'

'*Meeer*,' said Meer.

'*Ave Domitian!*' added Loquax.

'No tax on pets or personal belongings,' said the official. 'Only on imports and exports. Do you mean to sell any of your possessions?'

'No,' said Juba.

'Then you can go. Next!'

'Wait!' said Juba. 'We were hoping you might give us some information.'

The man sighed and leaned back in his chair. 'Not really my job,' he said. 'But I'll help if I can.'

'We're looking for our father's patron,' Juba said. 'He's of the equestrian class and his name is Lucius Domitius Pantera. Have you heard of him?'

The man pursed his lips. 'Isn't he the one who imports that fancy fish-sauce?'

'That's him!' cried Ursula.

Juba gave her a warning look and she pressed her lips together. 'We were told he has a big villa somewhere near Londinium,' Juba told the man.

'Pantera doesn't live near Londinium,' said the official. 'He lives down on the south coast. I believe he's just moved into the old governor's summer palace.'

'Where?' asked Juba. 'How far?'

'Place called Fishbrook,' said the official. 'About three or four day's walk from here. Or half a day by carriage.'

'Where can we find a carriage?'

The man jerked a thumb over his shoulder. 'Head west, cross the bridge and look for anybody taking goods to the south coast. If they have room they might let you ride for a few sesterces. Probably a bit late in the day now. Plus the games are on. Every Londoner apart from me is there now.' He sighed deeply.

'Where can we buy some goats' milk for my kitten?' Ursula asked.

The official shrugged. 'Maybe at a hospitium or inn. The town is full of them. The best ones are near the forum which you can always locate by the sound of hammers and saws. They're building a massive new basilica. Next!'

A moment later they were outside, blinking in the watery sunshine.

'Thank the gods,' whispered Juba 'We got past them.'

He took a deep breath of Londinium's air. It smelled of damp timbers, wood smoke and lye, with a hint of sickly sweet sewage.

He had just spotted a lofty scaffold rising above rooftops to the north when a barefoot girl in a blue and green chequered tunic ran up and grabbed his wrist. 'Please!' she cried. 'Your friend is hurt. You must come quickly!'

Juba narrowed his eyes at her. She spoke Latin with hardly a trace of an accent but she was obviously a Briton: reddish hair in a plait down her back, green eyes and a light dusting of freckles on her nose.

He pulled his arm away. 'What friend?' he asked warily.

'The boy with the black hair and cloak, and light brown tunic,' she said. 'He came off the same ship as you. Some men captured him and I think they're going to hold him for ransom.'

'Castor!' cried Ursula. 'She means Castor.'

Juba cursed and glanced around. 'We don't know this town,' he told the girl. 'We're just off the boat.'

'He's not far!' She pointed. 'He's in one of the big warehouses.'

'Why don't you tell one of the officials?' Juba asked. 'Or a soldier? There are two of them in the customs house.' He turned to go back inside when she caught his wrist again.

'They won't listen to me,' the girl cried, holding his gaze with pleading eyes. She lowered her voice so that only the three of them could hear. 'They hate me because I'm Boudica's great granddaughter.'

Chapter Twenty-Five
DOLIUM

Fronto stared at Boudica's great granddaughter.

With her leaf-green eyes, copper-coloured hair and freckled nose, she was the most exotic girl he had ever seen. She saw him staring and turned her long-lashed eyes on him.

'Will *you* help me?' she asked him.

Fronto tried to answer but his tongue refused to move. Sometimes this happened to him. He would be so amazed by something that he could not speak. Serapion, his tutor from Rome, often sneered, 'What's the matter? Have you been paralysed by the stars?'

Now he had been paralysed by the girl's sparkling green eyes, and could only nod dumbly.

'Oh, thank you!' She let go of Juba's wrist and took his hand instead. 'Come on!'

Still holding the birdcage in his left hand, Fronto let her pull him past shut up warehouses, piles of rubbish and stationary carts and waggons.

As the girl veered into a narrow alley, he glanced over his shoulder to see if the others were following. They were. Juba was scowling and Ursula looked worried. Meer clung to her shoulder.

Fronto wished he could touch a wall for good luck but he didn't want to let go of her hand and he couldn't drop the birdcage. Instead he muttered, '*Right, left, right. Right, left, right.*'

When they came out of the alley, they veered right onto a narrow unpaved street with shops and bars. It was like a smaller, muddier version of Rome. He had to jump over a pile of animal guts mixed with something worse and almost tripped over a small pig rooting in the gutter.

Without warning, the girl stopped by a wide shuttered doorway, glanced round and then pushed open the unlocked door on the right. Fronto stepped over the threshold with his lucky foot first. He followed her through a dim workshop full of animal hides and out into a bright courtyard. They were in a leather factory.

The strong smell of freshly tanned animal skins hit the back of his throat and he saw he was in a space filled with tubs of coloured liquid and piles of cowhides and sheepskins. The girl led him through tunnels made by tall stacks of skins. When she let go of his hand he felt like the hero Theseus in the middle of the labyrinth.

Finally the girl stopped and put her finger to her lips. In the silence they could hear faint groans. They were at one end of the smelly courtyard.

The copper-haired girl peeped round a pile of skins, then beckoned them forward.

Four huge clay jars were sunk into the ground almost to their lips. Three of them were full of foul liquid. The fourth dolium contained a boy, naked apart from a loincloth.

'It *is* Castor!' gasped Ursula.

'By the gods,' muttered Juba. 'Help me lift him out, Fronto.'

Fronto handed the birdcage to Ursula and bent to heave

Castor out of the empty jar. He had ugly bruises on his white thighs and ribs. There was blood on his mouth and his left eye was already swelling.

'Oh, Castor!' Ursula gasped. 'Someone beat you.'

Castor nodded weakly. 'Three robbers,' he muttered. 'They took everything. At least they left my loincloth.'

He was shivering so Fronto pulled off his dark brown cloak, which was woven in one piece with just a hole for the head and a sewn-on hood. 'Here,' he said. 'Wear this.'

'Thank you.' Castor winced as Fronto tugged the cloak over his head.

Juba rounded on the red-haired girl. 'How did you know where to find him? Were you part of this?' He looked around warily. 'Are your friends going to rob us, too?'

'No!' cried Boudica's great granddaughter, her face as white as the chalk cliffs they had passed three days before. 'But the men who did this will come back any moment. We have to get him out of here.'

Juba turned to Castor. 'Can you walk?'

Castor groaned. 'Not sure . . . I twisted my ankle in the struggle.'

He tried to take a step forward and almost collapsed, so Fronto put his arm round him.

'How do we get out of here?' Juba asked the British girl.

'This way.' Boudica's great granddaughter led them back the way they had come,

'Where are you lodging?' Juba asked Castor as they followed the girl. 'Do you have any friends or relatives here in Londinium?'

'My cousin might be here somewhere,' Castor slurred, 'but I'm not sure. I don't know where I'm staying, either. I had plenty of gold when I disembarked. But they took everything.'

'What's your name, girl?' Juba called out to the red-haired girl.

'They call me Bouda,' she said over her shoulder. They were back in the dim shop now.

'Do you know somewhere to stay near here, Bouda?'

'The Phoenix Hospitium is close by.'

'The Phoenix!' said Fronto. 'The one that man was telling us about. That's a good omen,' he added.

Back at the dim, wide doorway, Bouda put up her hand to stop them. 'Wait while I see if it's safe.' She pulled open the door next to the bolted shutters, peeped out, then beckoned them on.

Fronto and Juba helped Castor through the narrow night door. Ursula followed, with Meer on her shoulder and the birdcage in her hand.

As they emerged onto the street, Fronto glanced up and down. Apart from a passing oxcart and a woman leaning out of her window there was nobody around.

'You're being Good Samaritans,' Castor mumbled.

'What?' Fronto asked.

'Just a story the Christians tell.'

A few drops of rain began to fall, so Fronto pulled the hood of the cloak over Castor's head.

'Thank you,' said Castor. Then he groaned as Fronto and Juba helped him limp along a wooden walkway in front of the shops.

'The Phoenix hospitium is over there.' Bouda pointed. 'Just across the road. Put up your hoods,' she said to Ursula and Juba. 'In case anyone sees us.'

She held out her arm to stop them crossing and looked nervously left and right. 'All clear,' she said. 'Follow me.'

Chapter Twenty-Six
HOSPITIUM

Juba was relieved to find that the owner of the Phoenix Hospitium was a brown-haired Briton who had never heard of the chatty Phoenician man from the customs' shed; the fewer connections they made, the better their chances of reaching his uncle safely. But his brother was disappointed.

'Every third hospitium in Londinium is called the Phoenix,' the innkeeper explained to Fronto. 'Especially those that were rebuilt after the town burned down.'

Bouda tugged Juba's cloak and when he bent down she whispered in his ear. 'I'll help you get a good price for a room if I can stay with you and be your guide.'

'Don't you have a home?' he asked.

She shook her head and her lower lip trembled. 'I'm an orphan. I usually sleep in doorways. A real bed is all I ask for payment.'

'Can you help us find a carriage to the south coast tomorrow?'

'Of course!' she said, instantly brightening.

Juba turned to his sister. 'You don't mind sharing a bed, I hope?'

'With her?' Ursula looked shocked. 'I've never shared a bed in my life!'

The innkeeper snorted. 'You must have led a fine life if you've never had to share a bed. But I can bring up a folding camp bed if you don't like the idea of someone else's cold feet.'

'A camp bed like some army officers use?' Fronto's eyes lit up. 'May I have one, too?'

'If that's what you want.'

Juba nodded to the innkeeper. 'All right,' he said. 'I'll take a room for tonight.' He paid the man and turned to Castor. 'Can you make it upstairs?'

'Of course,' said Castor, his swollen lip making the words thick.

Ursula tugged the innkeeper's tunic. 'Do you have any goats' milk for my kitten?'

'I should be able to find some,' he said. 'Got any luggage apart from that birdcage? No? Then follow me.' He took a wooden frame with leather latticework from behind his table and started up the stairs.

As soon as he stepped over the threshold, Juba's heart sank. The room was dark and damp, with only one small window overlooking the street. The floor was at a slant, which made him feel dizzy. And the bed crunched when Castor sat on it.

'What's the mattress made of?' Juba asked the innkeeper.

'Straw, of course. Easier to keep it fresh. You wouldn't want fleas.' He was unfolding the wood and leather object, which turned out to be a low bedframe with a criss-cross of straps. 'Maybe you'd better put that lad on this camp bed. Easier to sponge off the blood. Chamberpot is under this table,' he added, tapping a chipped bowl with the toe of his boot.

When the innkeeper had gone, Ursula turned to Juba. 'We have to get some clothes and shoes for Castor,' she said. 'And milk for Meer.'

'But the shops are closed for the games,' Juba pointed out.

'I know where to get all those things,' Bouda offered. 'And which shops are open. But you'll have to give me some money.'

Juba gave her a sharp look. Beggars in Rome were skinny and grubby. This girl looked well fed and clean and her tunic had no patches or signs of wear.

'I'll go with you, if you like,' Fronto offered eagerly.

Juba sighed. He counted out fifteen silver coins, more than half the change from the gold aureus, and handed them to Fronto.

'I'm entrusting these to you, Fronto. It's a lot of money. Go with Bouda and buy Castor some boots and a tunic. A cloak, too, if you can afford it.'

'I know all the best places to buy clothes and shoes,' Bouda said. 'I can easily get all those things, plus a nice bunch of parsley to make a poultice for your friend's bruises.'

As Juba nodded, his stomach growled. 'All right,' he said. 'And if you have any money left over, buy us something to eat.'

Chapter Twenty-Seven
MILITES

'Where are we going?' Fronto asked Bouda, as she led him back towards the warehouses. 'The forum is that way. I can see the scaffolding for the new basilica.'

'It's cheaper to buy woollen cloaks directly from the warehouses,' she said over her shoulder.

'I thought they were all closed.'

'Not all. I know a cobbler near here who makes sheepskin boots. He won't be at the games.'

They picked their way across the muddy street, walked along a rough sidewalk of wooden planks and stopped at a narrow alley between two warehouses. Bouda glanced up and down the street.

Fronto wondered why she was so nervous. Perhaps she was afraid to be out after dark, for it was already dusk and the cloudy sky was a deep, vibrant blue. The narrow road was deserted except for a man lighting torches outside a tavern.

As soon the man went inside, Bouda backed into the alley and pushed a plank low in the wall. It swung to one side. 'In this way,' she said. 'Can you fit?'

'No,' Fronto said, feeling his face grow hot. 'I'm not as skinny as you.'

'Then give me the money,' she said. 'And wait on the boardwalk. When I come back, I'll knock on the wall three times. If there's nobody about, knock back twice, like this.' She gave two soft raps on the warehouse wall.

'All right.' Fronto handed over the fifteen silver coins and watched her disappear. When the board stopped swinging, it looked like all the others. He would never have guessed there was a way in.

As he stood on the street, it started to rain. He shivered. He should have got his cloak back from Castor or borrowed Juba's. At least he was wearing two tunics.

A noise made him start. It was the jingle of armour and the crunch of hobnail boots on a wooden walkway: the distinctive sound of Roman soldiers.

Two of them were coming along his side of the street. Had the Emperor's men finally caught them?

It was too late to run, so Fronto stood stock-still in the drizzle. *If I don't look at them they won't look at me*, he told himself. *Don't look. Don't look. Don't look.*

With his finger he nervously tapped the wall behind him: *right, left, right.*

Then he remembered a tap was the all-clear signal for Bouda. So he clenched his fists. The soldiers were almost upon him and it took every ounce of self-control not to panic.

Don't look, don't look, don't look.

The soldiers had almost passed when one of them stopped and turned to look at him.

'You all right, son?' he asked in accented Latin. 'You look like you just seen Medusa.'

'I am fine,' Fronto stared straight ahead. 'I am just fresh off the boat.'

'You look it,' said the other. 'Where's your cloak? You been robbed?'

'Not here in Londinium,' Fronto said. 'They tried to rob me in Rome but they couldn't get the ring off my finger.' He held out his hand to show them.

'Nice carnelian,' said one of the soldiers. 'And nice boots. Well, I wouldn't hang around by these warehouses, if I were you. This part of town is notorious for thieves and robbers.'

'Yeah,' said the other. 'There's one gang that uses a pretty girl as bait. She tells them she's lost her puppy or some such nonsense. Any fool who follows her into a warehouse gets robbed and beaten for his trouble.'

Fronto felt a sinking in his stomach.

'You got a place to stay?' asked the first soldier.

Fronto thought quickly. 'The Peacock Hospitium,' he lied.

'No such thing,' said Soldier Two. 'I think you must mean the Phoenix Hospitium. It's just up there.' He pointed back the way they had come.

'Yes. That's it. Thank you, sir.' Fronto turned and slowly walked away. But as soon as they were out of sight he hurried back to the warehouse with the loose board.

He felt the familiar taste of panic in his mouth. Juba had entrusted most of their remaining money to him. He should have stayed with Bouda.

Instead he had handed over the silver and was standing here like a fool.

Blood rushed to his cheeks, and he clenched his fists.

What would he tell Juba?

Chapter Twenty-Eight
PATINA

More than two hours had passed since Fronto had gone shopping with Boudica's great granddaughter, and Juba was worried.

It was now pitch dark outside and not much brighter inside. Their small bedroom in the Phoenix Hospitium was lit by an oil-lamp that sat on a small wooden table over a chamberpot. The innkeeper had charged another dupondius for the lamp. And he had charged a quadrans to refill Ursula's wineskin with goats' milk for Meer. Ursula was cradling the furry creature in the crook of her left elbow and letting her drink milk from the nozzle of the skin.

Juba got up off the bed and paced back and forth on the slanting floor, wondering what could be keeping his brother and the British girl. Had he been a fool to trust her?

A moment later Ursula cried.

'A mouse!' She scooped up Meer who had been exploring the floor.

'Where?' Juba picked up the clay oil-lamp. Its small flame made part of the room flicker spookily and plunged the rest into darkness.

'I thought you liked animals,' mumbled Castor from his

leather camp bed. His face had swollen badly in the past two hours and his lower lip was thick as a sausage.

'I do,' said Ursula. 'I don't want Meer to eat it. She chased a mouse in Rutupiae.'

Outside the room came the sound of creaking stairs, and Fronto's familiar voice.

Juba's brother and the British girl came smiling into the room.

'Why is it so dark in here?' Fronto asked. He was wearing a dark woollen cloak with the hood up.

'Innkeeper charges extra for oil-lamps,' Juba said. 'I could only afford one.' He looked at Bouda. 'Is that normal?'

She shrugged and then nodded. 'Olive oil for the lamps is expensive. But don't worry. Look what we bought for Castor: a tunic, a cloak and sheepskin boots with cosy lining.

Ursula narrowed her eyes at Bouda. 'I see you have a new cape and boots, too. Did you use our money to buy those?'

Bouda nodded and lifted her chin. 'I even had enough left over to buy food!' she held up a disc-shaped parcel wrapped in cabbage leaves and twine.

'Bread!' Juba cried, his stomach growling.

'Not bread,' Bouda said. 'It's something I've always wanted to try. It's called milk patina.'

'Milk patina?' echoed Ursula.

'Yes,' Bouda said. 'A patina is like a pie. Only a savoury one, not a sweet one. You put lots of things in with egg and milk and when you bake it the egg goes hard and holds all the other ingredients in.'

'We know what a patina is,' Ursula said. 'But I don't eat meat, only cheese and eggs . . . What's in it?'

Bouda's jaw dropped. 'You don't eat meat?'

'Ursula is the only one of us who doesn't,' Juba said apologetically. 'I eat meat.'

'Me, too.' Fronto's voice was muffled as he pulled off the charcoal grey cloak he had bought for Castor. 'What meat is in it?' he asked, as his head emerged.

Bouda's smile returned. 'It's got all the things you Romans love: chopped up oysters, sea urchins, pork sausage, chicken livers and boiled calf brain. There's also white celery, artichokes, cabbage, pepper, pine nuts and fish-sauce. And sheep's milk of course, which gives it its name. It's a luxury dish,' she added. 'I thought it would remind you of home.'

'Fronto!' wailed Ursula. 'How could you let her buy something like that? You know I don't eat animals. And you hate food that's chopped up and mixed together.'

Fronto shrugged. 'She said it would be tasty.'

'Did you say the sausages were pork?' Castor asked. 'We Jews can't eat pork. It is considered unclean.'

'I'm sorry,' Bouda said. Even in the dim lamplight, Juba could see her eyes were filling up with tears. 'I thought it would be a treat for you all.'

'We got honey cakes for desert,' Fronto held up his knotted napkin, 'You can have mine.'

Ursula glowered. 'Didn't you buy any bread?'

'We thought the patina and honey cakes would be enough,' Fronto said.

Ursula ignored him and turned to Bouda, 'Go get some bread now!' she commanded, pointing towards the door.

'I'm not your slave.' Bouda glared at them all. 'I was trying to help you! But you're just a bunch of rich, pampered Romans. You won't last a week in Britannia.'

'Bouda, wait!' Fronto called as she went out the door.

But the British girl had gone. They all heard her thumping down the stairs in her new boots.

'Good riddance,' Ursula said.

'I liked her,' Fronto said. 'We're lucky we met her and not that other girl or we might have been robbed and beaten like Castor.'

'What other girl?' Juba gave his older brother a sharp look.

'The one who tells passengers fresh off the boat that she's lost her puppy in a warehouse.'

'Puppy?' Ursula's face lit up.

'And when they follow her inside her friends beat them up and rob them.'

Ursula looked wide-eyed. 'Is that what happened to you, Castor? Did a girl ask you to find her lost puppy?'

Castor gave a weak smile. 'No,' he said. 'I was walking by a warehouse when I heard a woman scream. Or maybe it was a girl . . . I'm not sure. When I went to help, two strong men grabbed me from behind. I didn't even have time to cry out for help.'

'Wait a minute,' Juba turned to Fronto with a frown. 'Who told you about the girl and her friends who beat and rob people?'

'The soldiers.'

'Which soldiers?'

'Some soldiers on patrol. But they weren't after us. The soldiers in Ostia were different ones.'

'And who is the supreme commander of all soldiers in the Roman Empire?'

'The Emperor?'

Juba nodded grimly. 'The Emperor Domitian, our mortal enemy.'

Chapter Twenty-Nine
PRAETORIUM

S omeone was shaking Ursula awake.

It was Bouda. Ursula couldn't see her face but she could hear the panic in her voice.

'Soldiers are coming! Warn the boys! Quick!'

'What are you doing here?' Ursula said, groggily. 'Didn't you go away?'

'No! I was sleeping downstairs in a storage room. They're here right now! Talking to the innkeeper!'

But it was already too late. Ursula heard their hobnail boots loud on the wooden steps, their armour jingling, their voices deep.

As they came into the room, she shrank back, clutching Meer. She had seen soldiers before on the streets of Rome, but she had never been this close to them before. With their clanking armour, creaking leather and hairy legs they seemed to fill the small space. They smelled, too: of sweat, leather and socks.

'What's happening?' asked the boys sitting up on their cots.

'You three,' said one of the soldiers, almost cheerfully. 'Come with us.'

'You can stay,' the other one said to Castor. And to Bouda, 'You, too.'

'Give me your kitten,' Bouda whispered to Ursula. 'I'll protect her. And Loquax, too.'

'Thank you!' whispered Ursula. 'If anything happens to me, be good to her.'

As she followed her brothers down the stairs she reached into the neck of her tunic and brought out Canicula, her rabbit fur puppy. In the absence of Meer and Loquax, stroking him always gave her courage.

On the street, a few torches were still burning but already people were out and about. The soldiers led them north through the slowly brightening morning, then turned west onto a broad road. She stroked her toy puppy and considered making a run for it, but if she did they might punish her brothers.

Ursula glanced over her shoulder at Fronto walking behind her. He looked miserable.

'Are they the soldiers you saw yesterday?' she whispered.

He nodded.

'Shush!' said the soldier walking behind him, but he gave her a wink. Ursula was still confused, but his wink lifted her spirits and she began to look around.

Shopkeepers were pulling back shutters and stall-holders were setting up stalls. A man with a tray passed by shouting 'Fresh Bread!' in almost unrecognisable Latin. A moment later the scent of fresh baked bread made her stomach growl fiercely. She smelled fish as they passed the fishmonger's stalls.

Looking down a side street in the bluish light of early morning, Ursula saw the masts of boats; they were walking parallel to the river, on higher ground. The buildings were bigger here than down by the river. Most were plastered with half timbers showing. Then they passed a great temple on the higher ground.

The sun was up, but hidden by clouds, as they reached a grand arched entrance on their left.

A marble milestone stood there at the edge of the road and one of the soldiers patted it with his right hand before turning to lead the way through the arch. Ursula patted it, too, and saw Fronto's hand reach out to give it his usual *right, left, right.*

Ahead of them through the courtyard was a building as big as a temple. It was faced with plaster and had square columns, two either side of a big door guarded by sentries.

As they reached the guards, the soldier leading them said, 'Three to see the governor's scribe.'

The guard nodded and they entered a vast, high-ceilinged room big enough for a thousand men. Their footsteps echoed in the vast space as they made for a pearly square of light at the far end.

The square of light became a doorway leading into a big garden courtyard with trees, statues, fountains and a long pool with curved ends. The soldier led them across a circular pavement of coloured marble and past a splashing fountain to a columned walkway.

The sight of this opulent inner courtyard gave Ursula a pang of homesickness. She could almost imagine that she was back in Rome. The only thing wrong was the light. It was grey and soft, and cast no shadows.

The colonnade led them past fine rooms with frescoed walls. In one room seven children were sitting on benches listening to a grey-haired man chanting in Greek. They turned their heads and Ursula was surprised to see two of the children had skin the same colour as hers. But the soldiers hurried them past and the sound of poetry soon faded behind them.

At the end of the colonnade was a room with a heavy

red curtain drawn right back. It was lined with scroll-filled pigeonholes. In its centre stood a marble table covered with sheets of papyrus and wooden wax-tablets. Although it was morning, the bronze standing-lamps were lit and coals glowed in a bronze brazier.

'Oh, Hieronymus and Piso,' said a woman's voice. 'They look terrified. Didn't you tell them not to worry?'

Ursula and the others turned to see a young woman in a sky blue stola sitting by the side wall. The curtain had screened her until they came right into the study. The woman had a scroll in her lap and a woolly footstool at her feet. When she stood, the woolly footstool unfolded itself and stood, too. Ursula found herself face to face with the biggest, lankiest, curliest dog she had ever seen.

Ursula put away her toy puppy and stepped forward; this one was real. 'Oh!' she breathed. 'It's a pony dog!' She held out her hand, palm down, as her father had taught her.

The dog touched his cold black nose to Ursula's fingers. Then his tail gave a gentle wag and big panting pink tongue came out. It made his mouth seem to smile but his eyes still looked sad.

'Why does he have sad eyes?' Ursula asked the lady.

'Actually, he is a she,' said the woman, putting the open scroll on the desk. 'And she will be having her first litter in a few weeks. She's sad because a young friend of hers is missing.' The woman turned to the soldiers. 'Thank you, Hieronymus and Piso,' she said. 'You may go.' She gestured for them to sit on a couch by the wall.

With their backs against a black and cream fresco panel, the three of them looked out at the great pool with its two splashing fountains. The lady turned her wicker chair so she could face them. Her high light brown hair was curled in the front and plaited in the back. It was a fashionable hairstyle that took two slave girls at least an hour to do. Ursula knew because her mother had once had her hair done this way for an audience with the Emperor. The lady must be very rich to have such an expensive hairdo and such a big dog.

She must be clever, too, because she had been reading a scroll in Greek. Although Ursula could not read Greek, she knew the shapes of the letters.

Ursula watched the big dog settle herself back on the mosaic floor by the brazier.

'What's her name?' she asked.

Before the woman could answer, a young man appeared with honeycakes and mulsum on a tray. He passed round the tray so they could each take a honeycake, then put it on the desk so that he could pour out steaming cups of hot spiced wine.

They ate and drank gratefully while the woman stroked the dog's curly head. 'Her name is Cirrata,' she told them. 'And my name is Flavia Gemina. I am the wife of the governor's close friend and advisor. My husband and the governor are both in another part of the province on business, but sometimes I deal with certain matters on their behalf.'

Ursula gave some of her honeycake to Cirrata, who took it gently.

Flavia Gemina smiled at Ursula. 'You like animals, don't you?'

Ursula's mouth was full of honeycake so she just nodded.

'Are your cat and bird with you now?'

Ursula almost choked on her honeycake. 'How do you know I have a cat and a bird?'

Flavia Gemina's grey eyes were bright. 'I know because I am a detectrix.'

Chapter Thirty
PRINCEPS

Juba stared at the young woman. 'What is a detectrix?'

Flavia Gemina smiled. 'It's a word I coined myself. It means someone who uncovers the truth by observing clues.' She pointed to Ursula. 'One shoulder of your sister's cape has fresh bird droppings on it and the other is fluffed up with claw marks.' She turned to Ursula. 'I imagine you with a parrot on one shoulder and a cat on the other. Am I right?'

'A mynah bird and a kitten,' Ursula said, her eyes wide.

'That's incredible,' said Juba.

Flavia Gemina shrugged. 'Anyone can learn to do it. It's only a matter of looking carefully. I also know that the three of you are fresh off the boat and staying at the Phoenix Hospitium, correct?'

They looked at each other in amazement. 'How could you tell that?' Juba asked.

Flavia Gemina smiled. 'From two of my favourite soldiers,' she said. 'They told me they had met a dusky-skinned boy of about fourteen who said he was fresh off the boat and that he was staying at the Phoenix Hospitium. I presume that was you?' She looked at Fronto.

Juba rounded on Fronto. 'You told those soldiers where we were staying?' he cried.

Before Fronto could answer, Flavia Gemina said, 'Don't be angry with your brother. It's a good thing he talked to them. By the way, where is your baby sister?'

All the hair on Juba's neck rose up.

'How do you know about Dora?' he gasped.

The woman's expression was grave as she stood and went to the desk. She picked up a piece of official looking papyrus with part of a red wax seal still stuck to it.

'I know about you and your baby sister from this,' she said. 'It came last week for the governor. It is a warrant of arrest from our princeps, the Emperor Domitian.'

The papyrus crinkled as she unfolded it and read in a low voice, '*Wanted: children of the traitor Lucius Domitius Ursus and his wife Claudia Quarta, formerly of the Palatine Hill. The three children, two boys and a girl, have dusky skin and curly black hair and are possibly travelling with their baby sister. Their crime is treason and the theft of property belonging to the Princeps.*'

Juba clenched his fists. 'It's a lie!' he cried. 'The Emperor stole our property, not the other way round.'

'I believe you.' Flavia Gemina glanced around. 'The Emperor is no friend of mine. I have brought you here to warn you, and to offer my help. Nobody else knows. I am the only one who has seen this. And now . . .' She went to the three-legged brazier and dropped the document on the glowing coals. The warrant blossomed into yellow flames. They all watched the fire consume it.

Flavia Gemina turned back to them. 'For the moment you are safe. But if a duplicate warrant arrives, I might not be able to intercept it.'

'Why are you helping us?' asked Juba.

'Domitian is evil,' she said in a low voice. 'Because of him many of my family and friends had to leave Italia. But he is the most powerful man in the Empire and we must be careful. You should leave Londinium as soon as possible; his agents are everywhere. That's why I had the soldiers bring you so early. Do you have relatives or relations here in Britannia?'

Juba nodded and told her about their uncle on the south coast, three or four days by foot. He also gave her a brief account of their adventures.

'I've heard of Pantera,' said Flavia Gemina. 'But all I know is that he imports fish sauce and is very rich. What about your baby sister?' she asked. 'The one mentioned in the warrant.'

'I made the decision to leave her in safe hands in Ostia,' he said quietly.

'He didn't even ask me or Fronto,' Ursula scowled. 'But when Mater and Pater arrive with all their jewels,' she added, 'we can sail back to Ostia and get her.'

Juba clenched his jaw, willing himself to keep control of his emotions.

'Your brother made a very difficult choice,' Flavia Gemina said to Ursula. 'It's hard being the leader.' She looked at Juba keenly and he knew that she had guessed the truth. She really was a good detectrix.

He gave a tiny nod to express his thanks.

Flavia Gemina went to the tripod and poked the ashes of the Imperial message with a stylus. 'A carriage delivers wine and oil to the mansio in Noviomagus every Jupiter's Day,' she said. 'And one is going this morning. I can put you on it and you can travel . . . Oh!'

'What?' said Juba.

114

'I'm so foolish!'

'What?' they all said.

'Did you see the children in the room you passed to get here?' Juba and the others nodded.

'Two of them are the children of a dear friend of mine, my freedwoman Nubia. Last week, their little brother Audax disappeared. One moment he was playing in the courtyard, the next he was gone. A soldier found his toy chariot by the side of the river, near the bridge.'

She was pacing back and forth now, her dog watching with anxious eyes.

'Everyone said Audax must have drowned. But his mother and father refuse to believe he is dead. They have taken a boat downriver and are searching for him. And all the soldiers on patrol are looking for a missing toddler. But it's just occurred to me that he might have stowed away on the weekly mule-cart to Noviomagus. He loves carts and carriages ... And he disappeared a week ago today!'

She turned to look at them, her eyes bright.

'The cart goes to three official inns on the way to the south coast. Its last stop is just a few miles from Fishbrook, where your uncle lives. Will you keep your eyes open for any sign of little Audax? Your skin is the same colour as his. Perhaps you will spark someone's memory.'

'Of course, domina,' Juba nodded. 'We can do that. But how will we tell you if we hear of him?' he asked.

She thought for a moment and then cried, 'A winged messenger!' She clapped her hands and the young man who had brought the food appeared. 'Will you bring one of the carrier pigeons?' she said.

He vanished and came back with a square wicker cage

115

containing a plump pigeon. 'Do you see the ribbon round his foot?' said Flavia Gemina. 'If you find Audax or get word of him, write the name of the place on a piece of papyrus and attach it to him. Then release the bird into the air and he will find his way back here.'

'Really?' breathed Ursula. 'He can find his way back?'

'Yes,' said Flavia Gemina. 'In a matter of hours.'

'And if we reach my uncle with no notice of Audax?' asked Juba.

'Then send the bird back with the message that you have arrived safely. Now, which of you shall be his keeper?' She smiled, and placed the cage into Ursula's delighted hands.

III

Chapter Thirty-One
MULIO

Two hours after dawn, Ursula raced up the narrow stairs of the Phoenix Hospitium, taking them two at a time.

As she burst into the small room a voice said, '*Salve, Ursula!*'

'Loquax!' Ursula cried.

'I taught him that.' Boudica's great granddaughter stood in front of the small window. Her face was in shadow but the pearly morning light made her copper hair glow. She put down an apple core and picked up Meer. 'I've been training your kitten to hunt a piece of string,' she added.

'Thank you, Bouda!' said Ursula, taking Meer and putting her on her shoulder. 'Where's Castor?' she added.

'Here,' he said, coming into the room behind her. 'The innkeeper's wife was binding my ribs while Bouda was looking after your pets. We were about to go out looking for you. Are you all right?' he said. 'Where are your brothers?'

'They're waiting downstairs in the back of a mule-cart full of wine,' said Ursula. 'It will take us almost the whole way to Fishbrook, where our uncle lives.'

'I'm happy for you,' said Castor.

Ursula had an idea. 'Why don't you come with us?' she said. 'My uncle is rich. You can stay with us until your ribs are healed.'

'Really?' said Castor. 'Is there room in the cart?'

'Plenty!' said Ursula, trying to coax Loquax into his cage with the apple core.

Castor frowned. 'Will the driver mind?'

'No,' said Ursula cheerily. 'His name is Mulio and he's very nice. I'm riding up front with him but there's room in the back with the wine.'

'Can I come with you?' said Bouda. 'I can speak the language and be your guide.'

'We don't really need a guide.' Ursula stopped trying to get Loquax back in his cage and let him flutter up onto her right shoulder. 'As for speaking the language,' she said in Brittonic, 'we learned the basics on the voyage here. Didn't we, Castor?'

Castor gave her a crooked smile as he put on his new dark grey cloak.

'You have a strange accent,' Bouda muttered and then said in a louder voice, 'Please let me come with you? I want to get away from Londinium.'

Ursula was about to ask why when she heard the urgent clank of the mule-cart bell from downstairs.

'All right then,' she said. 'But we have to go now. Don't you have any other possessions?' she asked.

Bouda shook her head. 'I'm wearing all I own.'

'Me, too,' sighed Castor.

Outside it was cool and overcast. A big covered wagon hitched to four mules stood outside the Phoenix Hospitium. Ursula pulled back the flaps of canvas at the back. Juba and Fronto blinked at her. They sat on a bed of hay along with twenty big amphorae and the pigeon in its cage. 'Make room for Castor and Bouda!' Ursula laughed. 'They're coming with us to Fishbrook.'

Before her brothers could object, she ran to the front and clambered up onto the seat beside the driver.

Loquax fluttered up and then settled again as Mulio clicked with his tongue and the carriage rumbled into motion. The dull noise of iron-rimmed wheels got crunchier as the wagon turned off the dirt road and onto a road of densely packed gravel. It was the same road they had walked along at dawn but now it was crowded with men and women and all sorts of animals: mules, dogs, even pigs. The stall-holders were now shouting things like 'Sprats! Mackerel! Get them here!' and 'Oysters! Best from Rutupiae! Only two coppers for a dozen!'

They turned left before the Governor's Palace and headed downhill towards the river.

Ursula looked around happily. At last they were on the final part of their journey. She had her kitten on one shoulder and her bird on the other. And she was riding beside the driver.

Back in Italia, whenever they took their carruca to their Naples villa, her parents refused to let her sit beside the driver. It was not seemly, they told her, for a proper Roman girl to be seen next to a slave.

But she was sure Mulio was not a slave and it was so much nicer where she could see everything. She also loved watching the mules twitch their tails and ears.

Traffic slowed: there was a bridge up ahead.

'They're just waiting for a ship to pass through,' Mulio pointed. 'See? The drawbridge in the middle is just going down. That's the ship that went through.'

The mule-cart stopped and Ursula noticed some boys playing by the riverbank. It occurred to her that a child could climb up the back wheel and into the cart without being seen.

She turned to Mulio. 'You didn't see a little toddler last week, did you? With skin the same colour as mine?'

He shook his head. 'The lady asked me about little Audax and I told her it was unlikely that he could have ridden in my cart unnoticed.'

'But not impossible.'

'I suppose not. But if he'd stowed away I would have seen him when I unloaded the wine, wouldn't I?'

The carts and carriages were moving again and as they passed over the river, Ursula stood so that she could see better. The water was grey with a yellowish tint and there were lots of things floating in it, most of them unpleasant. She even saw the bloated body of a dead dog swirl past.

The cart jerked and she sat down with a bump. Startled, Loquax flew up off her shoulder and Meer said '*Meer?*'

Ursula scanned pedestrians and people in carts.

She could see ships and warehouses and people of many skin and hair colours, and seagulls overhead.

She could smell fish, smoke, sewage and most of all the scent of the river.

She could feel the breeze on her face and Meer's slight weight on her left shoulder, then a flutter as Loquax landed back on her right shoulder.

But there was no sign of a dusky-skinned toddler.

After crossing the bridge the cart moved along a high causeway between sheets of marshy water reflecting a soft grey sky. There were potteries and tanneries – she could smell them both – but only a few pedestrians. Although she knew she probably wouldn't spot little Audax here, she kept a sharp lookout.

She felt a nudge and heard Mulio's voice in her ear. 'Want to take the reins?'

Ursula nodded vigorously and took the leather straps.

'Why are you going to Noviomagus?' Mulio asked, once she had got the hang of it.

'We're actually going on to a place called Fishbrook where our uncle lives. Our parents might be there,' she added.

'I know the place.' Mulio scratched the rough grey tunic where it stretched over his stomach. 'Lots of fancy villas down on the south coast. Previous governor had a palace there. I had to bring him a load of fish sauce one time.'

'My uncle is an importer and exporter of fish sauce!' Ursula said. 'His name is Lucius Domitius Pantera. Do you know him?'

Mulio stared. 'Pantera? Does he import the Spanish fish sauce with the panther-fish seal?'

'That's him!' cried Ursula.

Mulio looked at her in awe. 'He's the owner of the palace now,' he said. 'You're going to be living with one of the richest men in Britannia! You'll have a life of luxury from now on.'

Ursula's heart soared. She had her kitten on one shoulder and her bird on the other. She was holding the reins of four wonderful mules taking her to an opulent new home, where her parents might already be waiting.

Then a sudden thought made her smile fade. She had told the cart-driver that Pantera was her uncle, not her father's patron. Had she just made a terrible mistake?

Chapter Thirty-Two
MANSIO

Drugged by the musty scent of wine, the rhythmic motion of the mule-cart and the deep rumble of iron-rimmed wheels on a paved road, Juba slept for the last stretch of the journey.

When the rumbling ceased and a sudden flood of bright light and fresh air filled the wagon, it took him a moment to remember where he was.

He saw Fronto yawning, Castor with his handsome but bruised face, and the pretty British girl called Bouda.

How strange that they now had travelling companions.

Maybe it was meant to be. Maybe this was the plan of the gods. Maybe he was meant to help others as Aeneas had saved his people. '*Save the children,*' his mother had told him that night.

He felt guilty that he had slept so long and not looked for little Audax.

Outside, at the back of the wagon, the driver was tying back the flaps of canvas. Ursula stood on the gravel forecourt.

'Did you see anybody who looked like the missing boy?' he asked her.

Ursula shook her head. 'We're going to ask the mansio-keeper here,' she said. 'Where's Palpito?' she said peering into the carriage. 'I can't see him anywhere.'

'Who?'

'Palpito. My pigeon.'

'Oh. I wedged his cage behind those amphorae so he wouldn't be too shaken. And it's not *your* pigeon. It belongs to the governor, for official business.'

'Where are we?' asked Fronto, stretching and yawning.

'We've reached the last mansio,' Ursula said. 'Mulio says it's only seven miles from here to Fishbrook.'

Mulio put up his hand to help Bouda off the back of the wagon. Juba jumped down and Fronto followed after touching the sides of the wagon: *right, left, right.*

Castor winced when he started to get up and pressed his hand to his side. Juba and the cart-driver helped him off the cart.

'Thank you,' Castor grunted.

'You're late today, Mulio!' A pot-bellied blond man in a celery green tunic came bustling up. 'It's almost dark. But all is forgiven as you've brought me a new lot of kitchen slaves as well as the usual wine.'

Juba stared at him in horror, then saw the man giving him a wink.

Bouda pointed towards the mansio. 'Is that a bath-house?' she asked. Juba saw steam rising from a white plastered dome behind the red tiled roof of the building.

'It most certainly is,' said the man, and scratched the armpit of his celery green tunic. 'We just had a couple of Imperial messengers through here about noon and they asked me to fire up the furnace for a session. They've left now, but it's still hot, if you want an hour's relaxation.'

'Yes, please!' Bouda clapped her hands. She looked at Juba.

'Can we girls go first?' She linked her arm in Ursula's so suddenly that Loquax flew up in the air.

The man in the celery green tunic laughed. 'For you and your bird I can do a session in the bath house plus dinner for one sestertius each.'

Ursula looked surprised, but pleased to have Bouda's arm through hers. 'That would be wonderful,' she agreed. 'I can't remember when I last had a hot bath.'

Juba frowned at his sister. 'We have to press on to Fishbrook.'

'But it will be dark soon!' Ursula said. 'We haven't bathed properly for over a month. It will only take an hour or so. We have to look nice for Uncle P–,' she stopped herself just in time. 'And I'm desperate for a massage.'

'Me, too,' said Fronto.

'That would take more than an hour,' Juba said. 'We'd have to have two sessions, one for you girls and one for us.'

The man in celery green tried again. 'For only a sestertius each I will give you two sessions in the bath-house, one for the girls and one for the boys, plus dinner, plus a room for the night. That way you can make an early start in the morning.' He gestured at Castor. 'And it will give this one time to heal from his session in the arena.'

'He's not a gladiator,' Fronto said. 'He got beaten up.'

'*Carpe diem,*' Loquax fluttered down onto Ursula's head. '*Carpe diem.*'

'He's a talkative one,' said the man.

'His name is Loquax,' Ursula said.

'*Salve, Loquax!*' said Loquax.

'Well my name is Exuperius and I am the manager of this mansio and this is my final offer: for only a sestertius each I will give you two sessions in the bath-house, one for the girls and one for the boys, plus dinner, plus a room for the night. Plus a hearty breakfast.'

'Do you have a proper sit down toilet?' Fronto asked.

'Indeed we do,' said the man. 'We have a four seater next to the bath-house.'

'Please can we stay here tonight?' Fronto asked Juba.

'Please?' Ursula and Bouda said together.

'Please?' Castor was rubbing his ribcage.

'*Please?*' echoed Loquax. He lifted his tail and a blob of white spattered onto Ursula's head.

'Oh no!' she cried. 'He got me! Now I *have* to bathe!'

Juba knew when he was beaten. 'All right,' he said. 'I suppose we should look our best for Unc . . . for father's patron. We've come this far. What harm could one extra night be?'

Chapter Thirty-Three
STRIGILIS

'I've been dreaming of this for six weeks!' said Ursula as she closed the door of the bath-house behind them.

Bouda looked puzzled. 'Where are the buckets?' she asked.

'This is only the changing room,' said Ursula. 'It's like the one in our villa in Rome.'

'You have a bath-house in your home?' Bouda gaped at Ursula. 'For just your family?'

'Yes,' said Ursula. 'We have bath-houses in both our villas.'

'You have two villas?' Bouda gasped. 'That's not fair!'

Ursula scowled. 'My father works hard.' But she felt a twinge of guilt as she reached down the front of her tunic for the ivory Venus.

As Bouda undressed, Ursula noted that her blue and green tunic was of good quality, but that she did not wear an undertunic. Her coin pouch was only cloth, but it seemed to be full and jingled when she put it on the shelf. Most surprising was what she wore on a leather thong round her wrist.

'Is that a *knife*?' gasped Ursula.

'Yes!' Bouda rolled it off over her hand and set it on the shelf beside her coin pouch. 'When you're an orphan beggar, Londinium can be a dangerous place. Oh look! Someone left a bottle of oil.' She picked up a globular glass bottle and pulled out the cork with her teeth. 'Ugh! She wrinkled her nose. 'It smells like turpentine.'

'It's terebinth,' Ursula said, giving it a sniff. 'My father's scribe wears this sometimes. He's a Greek from Alexandria.'

'Is terebinth expensive?'

'I don't know. Serapion isn't very rich, so probably not. What's that?'

'A strigil, I think. Put some oil on your body and I'll scrape you after.'

'Let's rinse ourselves first,' said Ursula.

They found some oversized wooden clogs and went from the warm changing room into the hot caldarium. It was a rectangular room with small open tanks at both ends and a shell-shaped marble fountain in the middle. The red bricks of the floor were arranged in a herringbone pattern; they were wet and hot.

Finding wooden buckets, they mixed hot water from the tank with cold water from the fountain until they got the temperature to their liking.

'You do me and I'll do you,' Ursula said, handing her bucket to Bouda.

Bouda carefully tipped a cascade of warm water over Ursula's head. 'Oh, that's wonderful!' said Ursula.

They sluiced each other half a dozen times, then Ursula dripped some oil onto the palm of her right hand and rubbed it over her arms, legs and trunk.

Bouda rubbed some on her body, too. Then they clumped over to a marble bench and sat in silence for a quarter of an hour, letting the steam do its work.

'Stand up,' Ursula suddenly commanded Bouda.

'I'm not your slave,' retorted Bouda, her cheeks pink.

'I know.' Ursula rolled her eyes. 'I'm going to scrape you.'

'Oh,' said Bouda and stood up. 'That's nice,' she added, as Ursula took the strigil and gently scraped the oil and sweat from her back.

'Where did the soldiers take you this morning?' Bouda asked after a few moments.

Ursula stopped scraping for a moment. 'What did Juba and Fronto tell you?' she asked cautiously.

'Juba said they took you because they were looking for a missing child with dusky skin like yours.'

'Yes.' Ursula resumed scraping, 'His name is Audax and he's only three. The clever wife of the governor's advisor asked us to keep an eye out for him. Now you scrape me.'

Bouda took the strigil from Ursula and began to scrape her back.

'Harder,' said Ursula. 'My slave girl never does it hard enough, either.' Bouda scraped more firmly. 'What was the lady like?' she asked. 'The wife of the governor's friend.'

'She called herself a detectrix,' said Ursula. 'That's someone who uncovers mysteries by looking for clues.'

Bouda stopped scraping so abruptly that Ursula turned. The British girl's face was bright pink.

'Could a clue be something like a little leather shoe?' asked Bouda. 'A little shoe that might fit a three-year-old?'

'Yes!' Ursula stared. 'Why?'

'Because I found one today, in the far corner of the carriage, right behind the amphorae.'

Chapter Thirty-Four
OLEUM

Fronto, Juba and Castor were sitting on a bench outside the mansio bath-house when the door swung open. The two girls stood there, dressed and with their cloaks around their shoulders, but with wet hair. 'Bouda found a clue in the mule-cart!' cried Ursula. 'Is Mulio still here?'

Juba shook his head. 'He started back right after you went in.'

Fronto stood up. 'What clue did you find, Bouda?' He thought she looked very pretty with her flushed cheeks and damp hair.

'A child's shoe. It was under the straw in one corner of the cart,' she said.

Castor had been stroking Meer on his lap. As he leaned forward with interest, Meer leapt onto Ursula and ran up her cloak as easily as a squirrel climbs a tree.

'Did you keep the shoe?' Castor asked Bouda.

'No. What would I do with one small shoe?'

'It doesn't matter that she kept it or not!' cried Ursula. 'It shows that Audax must have got a lift on that same cart last week! Where did you put Palpito? We have to send him to Flavia Gemina.'

'I put him in our room with Loquax, both in their cages,' Juba said. 'But let's wait a little longer before we send him. Maybe we can give her even better news. Maybe we can find the little boy.'

Fronto nodded. 'It's a sign from the gods,' he said. 'It's a good omen.'

'But how?' Ursula asked. 'How will we find him?'

'This mansio is on the main road,' said Bouda. 'Someone might have picked him up.'

'I don't think he's old enough to tell people who he is or where he's from,' said Ursula.

'We can ask along the way tomorrow,' said Juba. 'The innkeeper told me it's about seven miles from here to the south coast. Someone must have seen him.'

'But what if he went the other way? What if he went north?'

'I could go north,' said Castor slowly.

'No!' said Bouda and Ursula together.

Fronto had an idea. 'Let's ask the gods to show us a sign,' he said. 'They often speak to us by means of birds. Let's release Loquax from his cage. We'll ask the gods to make him fly in the direction the little boy went.'

'You'd better do it quickly,' said Castor. 'The sun is setting.'

Ursula ran to get Loquax, who was sleeping in their room. While they waited, Fronto moved closer to Bouda. Something about her was different.

He leaned forward and sniffed.

'What are you doing?' Bouda took a step back.

'You smell strange,' he said. 'You smell like Serapion.'

'What's Serapion?'

'Not what; who,' corrected Juba. 'Serapion is our father's secretary.'

'And our tutor,' added Fronto. 'He's been teaching us Greek.'

132

'That smell brings back bad memories,' Juba added. 'He used to mock us if we didn't get everything exactly right.'

'Well, it doesn't bring back bad memories for me,' said Bouda. 'I like it. Someone who was here before left a bottle of oil behind.' She held it up.

'They say terebinth is good for bruises and sore muscles,' said Castor, standing up slowly.

Fronto saw her cheeks go pink. Then she held out the bath-set. 'Then you have it! You need it more than I do.'

Ursula appeared, running across the gravel courtyard with Loquax flapping in the swinging cage.

'Careful!' cried Fronto. 'Don't upset him. We need him to be calm.'

Ursula nodded, gasping for breath.

Fronto took the cage and put it on the bench. 'Get out your gods,' he said, pulling Jupiter Ammon from inside his tunic. He put the little bronze figure on the bench beside Loquax. Juba and Ursula put their gods beside Jupiter.

Fronto put up the hood of his cloak and waited for the others to be silent. When it was quiet enough for him to hear the evening cheep of a blackbird and the breeze in his ears, he prayed out loud. 'Father Jupiter, clever Mercury and merciful Venus,' he said. 'Make Loquax fly in the direction the little boy named Audax went. If you help us we will give you half the reward.'

'Reward?' he heard Bouda whisper. 'You didn't tell me there was a reward!'

'Shhh!' said Fronto sternly. 'No sound must intrude, or it won't work.'

When they were quiet he picked up the cage and said again, 'Show us, O gods, which way to go. Give us a sign.' Then he opened the door.

Loquax remained firmly on his perch.

'Show us which way to go.'

'*I'm not scared; I'm excited!*' said Loquax, but he did not budge.

'Come *on!*' Fronto banged the side of the cage opposite the open door.

'*Ave, Domitian!*' Loquax flapped on his perch. '*Ave, Domitian!*'

'Don't!' cried Ursula. 'He doesn't want to go. He must be tired. He's been flying all day.'

Fronto felt a sense of dread. He had not expected this.

From some trees nearby came the blackbird's warning call: three silver chips of sound, a pause and three more. Then Castor silently pointed up. Black against the fading sky was a silently soaring bird.

'Falcon,' said Castor. 'Probably on his way home to roost. They take feathered prey,' he added, and his words sent a shiver through Fronto.

'That's why he didn't go out!' breathed Ursula, carefully taking the cage and closing the door. 'If he had gone out that falcon might have killed him!'

Fronto shuddered. Was the falcon the sign he had asked for? And if so, was it a good omen, or bad?

Chapter Thirty-Five
FAX

Juba woke late in the night. He had been having his usual nightmare, dreaming about what he had seen when the Emperor's men came.

He lay quietly, letting his heartbeat return to normal and listening to the sound of the rain. Fronto was snoring, and so was one of the girls.

From his right came a low voice: Castor's. 'Did you hear that?'

Juba pushed himself up on one elbow, frowning. 'What?'

'Someone banging at the front door of the mansio. I'm going to have a look.' His leather cot creaked. The tiny flame of the night-light showed his dark shape limping to one side of the window.

'There are two horses out there,' Castor said in a low voice. 'And two men in the porch. One is tall and thin, the other short and stocky.'

Juba was out of bed in one motion and bending over Fronto. 'Wake up, Fronto,' he whispered. 'You, too, Bouda. Ursula, we have to go *right now*. There are men outside, with horses. Be as quiet as you can.'

Ursula sat up, kissed her kitten's nose and placed the creature on her shoulder. Like Juba, she had slept fully dressed.

Bouda yawned and Fronto blinked groggily. A soft tap on the door made them freeze. Before they could do anything, the door opened and a grey-haired woman peered round. 'Men seek you!' she hissed in bad Latin. 'Exuperius he say you go now! There is path, behind bath-house!'

Juba led the way into the corridor.

Memories of that terrible night a month earlier came flooding back.

He found the narrow stairs and heard the others creaking after him.

It had been raining and a pine-pitch torch in the courtyard showed puddles everywhere. Milky clouds raced across a dark sky. A half moon shone like a deformed pearl.

Juba led the way round a wooden table and stifled an oath as he banged his shin on a bench underneath it. He limped between buildings to an open space flanked by the bath-house on one side and the stables on the other. A whiff of hay and horses made him wish they knew how to ride.

High above, the half moon slipped behind a cloud and the night became darker. He glanced over his shoulder. 'Ursula?'

'I'm here,' came his sister's voice. 'Right behind you.'

'I'm here, too,' Bouda said.

'Me, too,' said Castor.

'Right, left, right!' whispered Fronto from the rear.

'Good!' Juba hissed. 'Now be quiet until we reach the bath-house.'

When they reached the bath-house they groped their way round to the back of it.

'Do you see the path?' came Castor's voice.

'No,' Juba whispered. 'It's too dark. We'll have to wait for the moon to come out.'

They brought their five hooded heads together to confer. Juba was between Castor and Ursula. Beneath hair and wool, he could feel the reassuring solidity of their skulls pressed against his.

'Why do they always come at night?' Ursula whispered.

'Because it's when we are most helpless,' Castor replied.

'Who are they?' whispered Bouda. 'Did you see them?'

'I'm not positive,' Juba said. 'But I think it's the Emperor's henchmen.'

'You're running away from the Emperor?' gasped Bouda.

'I'm afraid so,' Juba admitted. 'We should have told you earlier.'

'What do they want from you?' Bouda asked.

'We have no idea,' said Juba. And then, 'Shhh!'

They fell silent.

For a moment they could only hear the drip of rainwater from branches and eaves. Then they heard the voice of Exuperius, the mansio-keeper. 'I told you,' he whined. 'A bunch of kids went by around noon riding in a dung cart. They looked like they might be going to Cantiacorum or Portus Dubris.'

'How could you tell that?' A man's rough voice.

'That's what the cart-driver said.'

'And what did you say the cart-driver's name was?'

'No idea. He wanted a jar of wine so I sold him one.'

'If we find out you're lying then you'll regret it.'

Ursula held her breath. Meer meowed from her shoulder, '*Meeer?*'

'By all the gods!' Juba hissed in her ear. 'Shut that thing up!'

Ursula put down the bird cages, found the milkskin, uncorked it with her teeth and held it up for her kitten. It did the trick.

Juba's heartbeat had just returned to normal when Castor's voice said, 'Someone's coming. I see a torch!'

Juba had a sudden thought. If the Emperor's men found an imperial pigeon, it might lead them back to Flavia Gemina. Quickly he bent, pulled back the cloth over Palpito's cage and opened the door.

Unlike Loquax, the pigeon did not hesitate. Out he flew, and up. His fluttering wings were lit by the flickering yellow torchlight and then he was gone, swallowed up in darkness.

'Why did you do that?' Ursula squealed in a whisper.

'Shhh!' Juba hissed. He could see the elongated shadows of two figures coming round the bath-house. He quietly retreated, leading the way around the circular building in the other direction. There was nowhere else to go. If they went out in the open, they might be spotted.

The thing Juba most dreaded had come to pass. The Emperor's henchmen had followed them all the way to Britannia and tracked them down at last.

Chapter Thirty-Six
BACULUM

Ursula sensed the man behind her before she heard the crunch of his boot on gravel. She filled her lungs for an almighty scream when a meaty hand covered her mouth. She could taste something bitter on it and nearly gagged. 'Keep quiet!' hissed the mansio keeper. 'Or they might hear! They weren't after you, anyways,' he added, releasing Ursula. 'They were after her!'

The innkeeper was pointing at Bouda. His wife held up the flaming torch to show Bouda's pale, wide-eyed face.

They all stared at her in astonishment. 'Why are the Emperor's men after you?' Juba asked.

Bouda hung her head. 'They're not the Emperor's men. They work for Tyranus. One of them must have seen me get into the wine wagon.'

'Tyranus?' Castor frowned.

Bouda nodded. 'The leader of the East End Gang.'

'East end of what?' asked Juba.

She rolled her eyes. 'Londinium, of course. Tyranus controls the east part of the town and Fortis controls the west.'

Exuperius sucked in his breath. 'I've heard of them,' he said. 'They're a bad lot. Why are they after a pretty little thing like you?'

Bouda pointed at Castor. 'Because of him. I was supposed to be watching the warehouse until they came back, but instead I ran to get help.'

'But they'd already beaten and robbed him,' Juba said. 'What more would they want?'

Bouda looked at Castor. 'I don't know. Maybe they were going to hold you for ransom,' she said. 'They're after me because I helped you escape.'

'That means they're after you, too!' Ursula said to Castor.

The moon emerged from behind a cloud.

'Best you all move on, in that case,' said Exuperius. He pointed at a faint track in the moonlit grass. 'There's your sheep trail. Follow it for a mile or two and you'll come to a little village of round huts and four-horned sheep.'

'Four-horned sheep?' echoed Ursula.

'Yes, indeed. Once you get to the village all you have to do is find the road southwest and follow it till you reach the sea. Here's your bird,' he said, handing the cage to Ursula. 'And you, lad.' He turned to Castor. 'Take this walking stick. You paid for a whole night. It's only fair. Now go on. Off you go.'

During their escape from Rome the night had been warm and balmy, full of creaking insects and the clop of mule hooves or grinding of wheels on stone.

This night-time world was completely different. It was cool and silent, with long, wet grasses over land that was neither flat nor hilly but something in between. The air felt cold in Ursula's lungs and the scent of it made her giddy, like the time she had finished half a goblet of her father's wine.

She dropped back to keep pace with Castor, who was following bravely with the help of his new walking stick.

It seemed they had been travelling for hours when the black

night finally gave way to the vibrant peacock blue of dawn.

They were making their way through a grove of silver birch, when a bird started to trill. Then another joined it and another and another.

Soon the air was full of birdsong: trills, warbles, shouts and flutings of joy. Thick as pepper, sweet as honey, the cascade of notes washed over and around her. She felt her spirit lifted up to the tops of the trembling trees. The others had stopped, too. Beside her, Castor lifted his face to the sky. On her left shoulder, Meer began to meow. She felt Loquax moving in his cage and she pulled off the coverings so he could be part of this miracle of nature and sing if he wanted to.

But like her, he was silent in the power of such magic.

Chapter Thirty-Seven
COHORS

When the dawn chorus finally faded to a few cheeps, Fronto said, 'Shouldn't we be going south?'

'Yes,' said Juba.

Fronto pointed. 'The sun is rising there. I think we've been going the wrong way. We should have reached the village or the road by now.'

Castor groaned. 'I don't think I can go much further. My ribs hurt like Hades.'

'You're white as chalk,' cried Ursula. 'You should rest.'

'Hush,' said Fronto. 'Do you hear that?'

'Hear what?' they asked.

To Fronto, it sounded like faint ghostly footsteps. But he knew better.

'Soldiers!' he said. 'I think it might be soldiers.'

'I hear it!' said Bouda.

'If there are soldiers,' said Juba, 'there must be a road!'

Fronto led the way through green shrubs, down into a grassy dip and up into another copse of trees.

'Look!' cried Ursula. 'I see a village!' She pointed to a clearing with seven round buildings. They had conical thatched roofs and rose from ground mist like strange pointed mushrooms. Nearby

142

Fronto saw fenced enclosures with sheep, goats, cattle and pigs.

'The road is the other way,' he said, pointing across a misty field of barley to a line of trees.

'Can't we go to the village?' Ursula said. 'I want to see a four-horned sheep. And their houses are round, just like the sailors told us.'

'We're on the run for our lives!' said Juba. 'We can visit a British village once we're safe at Uncle Pantera's. Lead on, Fronto.'

'Wait!' Castor was leaning on his staff. He looked at Ursula. 'Remember I said I lost my brother when I was little? He was kidnapped from Ostia. I grew up never knowing him. Then, last month, a sailor told me he had seen my brother in a village with round houses here in Britannia.'

'All British villages have round houses!' said Bouda.

'Yes, but I've got to start looking somewhere and it might as well be here. That's why I've been learning the language and customs. I will ask for salt and shelter. Nantonius told me that no village will refuse a guest who asks for those things.'

'But what about Tyranus's men?' asked Juba.

'I doubt they're still after me,' said Castor. 'I have no family in this province and no possessions. Besides, what better place to hide than a small village like that one? You go on,' he continued. 'When my ribs and sprained ankle have healed, I will come to your uncle's villa.'

Fronto was surprised to see his sister and Bouda almost in tears. He held out his hand and said, 'Gods go with you.'

'And you,' said Castor. He shook Fronto's hand and then turned to Juba. 'I am sorry for being so hard on you,' he said. 'I hope you can forgive me.'

'Of course,' said Juba gruffly. 'Go with your god.'

'Goodbye Castor!' Ursula threw her arms around him for a hug. Meer meowed and Castor winced, but he was smiling when she let go.

Bouda stood on tiptoe and boldly kissed his cheek.

And then he was gone, limping down the grassy slope to the village. As barking dogs brought villagers out of their huts, Fronto and the others crouched behind shrubs. They saw an old man with a white beard and a gold torc come forward, and they could clearly make out his smile of welcome from their hiding place.

Before Castor disappeared inside the biggest roundhouse, he half turned to give a nod and a smile in their direction.

Everyone was subdued as they followed Fronto down a path beside the barley field towards the road. As they got closer to the trees, the sound of marching feet grew louder. Moving forward at a crouch, Fronto gestured for the others to do the same.

Soon they could hear the soldiers' marching song: *left . . . left . . . left, right, left!* Fronto could see the glint of their metal armour through gaps in the trees.

They reached the cover of roadside shrubs just as the final cohort approached. The crunch of their boots made a rhythmic beat on the gravel-packed Roman road as they marched past.

Many of them wore chain mail shirts over long tunics. And almost all had brown skin.

'They're not regular legionaries,' Fronto said in Juba's ear. 'It must be a century of auxiliary archers. You can tell by their oval shields and their bows and arrows.'

'Maybe they're Parthians,' Juba said.

'Syrian, more like,' said Fronto. 'Parthians usually ride.'

As the column passed, Juba turned to the others.

'Let's fall in behind them!' he said. 'I don't think the Emperor sent a whole century just for us. And people will think twice about trying to hurt us if there are soldiers nearby. Put your hoods up and keep your heads down.'

Fronto was first to jump the rainwater ditch and turn onto the road. He could still see the backs of soldiers with their shiny helmets, packs and covered oval shields.

The soldiers had been chanting a song. '*Awake and beware, for the Briton is near. He is laying an ambush to cut off your rear.*'

Fronto grinned as they started chanting a variation: '*Awake and beware, for some children are near. They're laying an ambush to cut off our rear.*'

But his grin faded a mile or two later, when Juba tugged his cloak and said in his ear. 'I still don't think we're going the right direction!'

Juba pointed to a lone building by the side of the road. It had a gravel forecourt with tables and benches, and a crudely painted wooden sign showing a blue cockerel. 'Let's ask for directions at that tavern.'

Fronto felt a pang of regret as they stopped at the tavern. He had enjoyed marching behind the soldiers.

One of the archers turned his head and gave them a cheery salute.

Fronto waved back and watched until they were out of sight. Then he went to join the others at one of the tables.

'Thank goodness!' Ursula had taken off her left boot and was rubbing her foot. 'I think I've got a blister.'

'Me, too,' said Bouda.

'You can't sit here unless you pay to eat or drink,' said a serving girl. She wore a chequered tunic of orange and rusty-red. Her hair was mahogany, a few shades darker than Bouda's.

'Have you seen our little brother?' Ursula asked. 'He's only three and he went missing a week ago.'

Fronto grinned. That was clever.

'Sorry,' said the girl, her expression softening. 'Haven't seen any stray kids.'

'We're also looking for Fishbrook,' Juba said. 'Are we on the right road?'

'You missed one turning a couple of miles back,' she said. 'But if you carry on another half mile the road forks. The track on the right, heading southwest, will take you to Fishbrook. Now, are you going to order?'

The thought of food cheered Fronto. 'What do you have?' he asked.

'Porridge to eat,' she said. 'Beer or whey to drink.'

'I've heard of beer!' cried Fonto. 'It's a specialty of this province,' he explained to Ursula. 'It's made with barley, not grapes!'

Bouda laughed. 'Haven't you ever tried it?'

Fronto shook his head.

'Then now's the time,' she replied.

'For breakfast?' said Fronto.

'Why not?'

'All right. Anybody else?'

Juba shrugged and then nodded. 'Five bowls of porridge, two beers and three beakers of whey,' he told the serving girl.

They cooled their hot feet in silence until the serving girl returned with their food. She put down five bowls of oat porridge and a clay jar of fish sauce. 'I'll be back with your drinks in a moment,' she said.

Before she could go, Ursula held up the clay jar of fish sauce. 'Don't you have the good stuff?' she asked.

'What good stuff?' asked the serving girl.

'The fish sauce with the sign of the sea-panther, of course. Our uncle imports it.'

The serving girl's eyes grew wide. 'Your uncle is Sea-Panther?'

'Yes,' Fronto said proudly. 'Our uncle is Lucius Domitius Pantera. Have you heard of him?'

With a violent movement of her arm, the girl swept the bowls full of porridge from the table and onto the ground.

Then she spat in Fronto's face.

Chapter Thirty-Eight
PARDALOCAMP

With their stomachs still empty and Fronto repeating the words 'bad omen' over and over, Juba led the four of them southwest towards Fishbrook.

Apart from Fronto's muttering, they walked in silence. Juba knew they were as tired, hungry and footsore as he was.

But the road was fine and the sky was a cloudless blue. The sea shone like a ribbon of grey above mottled green marshland. Golden fields of grain lay on their right. Seagulls hung in the air above them for a while, then wheeled off towards the south.

Fronto fell back a few paces.

'Why did she do that?' he asked his brother. 'Why did she spit in my face?'

'I don't know,' Juba said with a sigh. 'Maybe Uncle Pantera's fish sauce is too expensive for them.'

'It's expensive because it's the best,' said Ursula.

'Maybe she's jealous because he's rich,' said Juba.

'You never said he was rich,' said Bouda.

'He's so rich he lives in a palace,' said Fronto.

'A palace?' breathed Bouda.

'Yes, a palace!' snapped Juba. 'Is money all you care about?'

'No.' Bouda pointed. 'I meant a palace like that?'

Juba followed the line of her finger.

A slight bend in the road and a gap in the shrubs showed a massive villa up ahead. With its cream columns, red tiled roof and temple-like entrance, it reminded Juba of the Emperor's new palace just up the hill from their house.

'Oh, well done, Bouda!' cried Ursula. 'That must be it!'

Meer meowed in alarm as Ursula put down the birdcage, grabbed Bouda's hands and spun in a circle of joy.

'We're here!' she cried, and bent to open Loquax's cage.

'Don't get your hopes up,' said Juba, as Loquax went flying into the sky. But his own spirit was soaring with the bird.

'He knows where to go,' said Fronto. 'That must be a good omen.'

As they hurried after the bird, Juba could see Medusa's face staring at them from a triangular pediment above six columns. Her grinning face with its bulging eyes and stuck-out tongue was flanked by two painted sea creatures. On the left was a hippocamp, with the front of a horse and the twirly tail of a sea serpent. And on the right was a pardalocamp: half leopard, half fish. It was the sign on all the small jars and big amphorae of his uncle's fish sauce: the sign of the Sea Panther.

'Look!' Fronto pointed. 'Uncle Pantera's symbol! See it?'

'Yes!' Ursula squealed, and did another dance.

But Juba did not dance. As they approached the grand entrance of the palatial villa, something about it made his stomach twist.

Perhaps it was the serving girl's reaction when they had mentioned his uncle's name.

Or maybe it was because they had come so far and lost so much. He thought of his father's deep laugh, his mother's loving smile and his baby sister's gurgle of delight.

A sturdy wooden bridge took them over a stream that flowed south to an inlet. Juba saw two ships anchored there.

'That must be the brook this place is named after,' Ursula said, running to lean over the rail. She put down Loquax's empty cage, plucked her kitten from her shoulder and held her over the water. 'Look, Meer! Fish!'

As they covered the last few feet of the approach, Loquax fluttered down onto Ursula's right shoulder.

Juba could make out massive double doors, with long marble benches either side. As his tired feet brought him nearer, he saw two blond British men in pale yellow tunics and leggings sitting on one of the benches playing dice.

One of them glanced up and said something to his companion. They both grabbed spears leaning against the wall and stood to attention either side of the impressive double door.

Juba greeted them in Brittonic as he led the others up five marble steps.

The blond guards did not reply. They were young but muscular. Both had shaggy manes of yellow hair and droopy moustaches.

'*Salvete!*' He tried Latin, but they continued to stare straight ahead with fierce blue eyes.

'They're guards,' said Fronto. 'They're not allowed to talk.'

'I know that!' hissed Juba, reaching for the knocker. 'It's just that I've never seen British guards on such a Roman-looking villa.'

'It's not a villa,' said Bouda. 'It's a palace!'

Juba was still holding the bronze knocker but had not yet rapped.

'Knock!' urged Ursula. 'Meer's starving and so am I!'

Pushing away his feelings of apprehension, Juba took a deep breath and gave the door three smart taps.

He was suddenly aware how grubby they must seem in their dusty travelling cloaks and muddy boots. His father's lumpy woollen cloak – once the colour of a tawny lionskin – was now the sickly yellow of whey. Ursula's pine-green cloak had bird droppings on the right shoulder and a kitten on the left.

Dirt had made Fronto's cherry red tunic red-brown and dust had turned his cloak from acorn brown to mud brown.

Bouda looked the best of them. Her blue cape set off her copper hair and the sun had given her a pretty flush.

A panel opened at eye level and someone peered out. Juba took an involuntary step backwards at the sight of the whitest face he had ever seen. The man's eyes were colourless, with pink rims. The skin around them was chalk white. He even had white eyelashes.

'Yes?' said the pale-faced man. 'What do you want?'

Juba stood a little straighter. 'Is this the villa of Lucius Domitius Pantera?'

'It is.'

Juba exhaled with relief. 'My name is Lucius Domitius Juba,' he said. 'This is my brother Fronto and my sister, Domitia Ursula. Pantera is our uncle.'

'*Meeer?*' said Meer on Ursula's left shoulder.

'*Ave, Domitian!*' said Loquax from her right.

The man slowly blinked his pale eyes, then turned them to Bouda. 'And that girl?' he asked.

'Our guide,' Juba said. 'A British girl named Bouda.'

The man gave a small nod. 'Please take a seat,' he said. 'My master is in the baths, and will see you when he's finished.'

It was a relief to sit on one of the cool marble benches and rest their tired feet. When one of the massive doors swung open, they all jumped up.

The pale-skinned, white haired steward stepped out onto the porch. His cream linen tunic came to mid-calf, exposing white lower legs and unbleached linen slippers. Framed against the dark walnut of the door, he looked like an unpainted marble statue.

'The master will see you shortly,' he said. 'In the meantime, here is some cream for your kitten.' He stepped aside as a small blond slave boy set down a red bowl of cream.

Meer had been investigating one of the guard's boots, but when she smelled the cream she leapt for the red saucer like a tiny tiger attacking its prey.

The blond slave boy looked at Juba with a slight frown. But when he saw Bouda his eyes opened wide. He hissed something in Brittonic.

His accent was different from that of the sailors, but Juba caught the sense of it.

'Get out of here while you can! This is a bad place for people like you!'

Chapter Thirty-Nine
STATUA

The pale man smacked the slave boy on the ear. 'Go back inside at once!' he said, 'or I'll tell Fortunatus to give you a good beating.'

The boy ducked his head and scurried back inside.

The man with the white eyelashes turned to the children. 'My name is Albinus,' he said. 'I am your uncle's steward. Please follow me.'

Juba let Fronto go first. He noticed that Bouda followed his brother's lead; not only did she carefully step over the threshold with her right foot but she also touched the door frame: *right, left, right.* They were now in a large marble hall with alcoves, mosaics, a fountain and a tantalising glimpse of bright green gardens ahead. The black and white mosaic floor had a pattern of diamonds and squares. He shivered again.

Bouda was looking around with wonder in her eyes. 'This is an amazing house,' she breathed.

'You do realise,' said Albinus coolly, 'that this is just the entryway.'

Bouda trailed the tips of her fingers in the crystal-clear water in a marble-lined tank big enough to bathe in.

The steward nodded. 'This palace used to belong to

Togidubnus, a Briton who loved all things Roman,' he said. 'Then Governor Lucullus lived here. After Domitian executed him last year, Lucius Domitius Pantera acquired it.'

Juba looked up sharply, 'Domitian executed the governor of Britannia?' he asked.

Albinus nodded. 'For treason.'

Juba was about to ask how Domitian had killed the governor when they emerged from the huge entry hall into the bright open space of a vast garden surrounded by the red tile roofs and marble columns of the palace.

They stared in wonder. Two vast grassy rectangles lay before them on either side of a central pathway. On their right and left were trellises covered with grape vines. Loquax fluttered off Ursula's shoulder to investigate.

'Look!' Bouda pointed. 'They've cut the plants to make them look like benches or little walls! I've never seen such a thing before. And what are those two strange trees? They're so tall and thin and dark!'

'The hedge is boxwood,' Albinus said. 'And the trees are cypress. In another courtyard we have a small orchard and a garden with onions, chives, parsley, garlic, aniseed, fennel, coriander, mustard, dill and thyme.'

'It reminds me of home,' Ursula said, looking around.

'We could almost be back in Italia.' Fronto lifted his face to the warm sun.

'Is this what Italia looks like?' Bouda breathed.

'Yes,' Fronto said. 'Especially on an afternoon like this, with a high blue sky above red roofs.'

Ursula pointed to fountains lining the central path. 'The sunlight looks like Italia, too. The way it slants in and makes the water all sparkly.'

As Albinus led them along the path that bisected the gardens, Juba realised they were facing west, for the afternoon sunlight was directly in their eyes.

The sound of snipping brought his attention to two fair-haired slaves in unbleached cream tunics; they were crouching beside the hedge using sharp-edged shears to trim it.

'*Ah-OW! Ah-OW!*' To Juba's right, a peacock unfurled his tail-feathers in a dazzling fan.

'What is that?' breathed Bouda.

He heard Fronto say, 'That's a peacock.'

'Are they expensive?' she asked.

'Very,' he replied.

There was something strange up ahead. At first glance it looked like a soldier standing on a plinth. Juba knew it must be a statue, but the creamy marble skin was so expertly tinted and the breastplate, tunic and cloak so realistically painted that it sent a shiver down his back. It reminded him of the living statues at a party his parents had hosted the previous year. They had hired actors and actresses to wear starched garments and paint their faces to look like sculptures.

Juba stopped and squinted up at the statue. Something about it made the hairs at the back of his neck prickle.

The man had a high forehead, large deep-set eyes and a strong nose. Despite a firm chin, his petulant mouth wore a girlish pout. Juba realised where he had seen that face before.

'You know who that is, don't you?' Albinus said.

Juba nodded bleakly. 'The Emperor Domitian.'

'Yes,' replied Albinus. 'They say the resemblance is striking.'

Juba tried to swallow but his throat was dry.

Taking a deep breath to steady his courage, he followed the others as they mounted the steps of the temple. *Was Uncle*

155

Pantera a friend of Domitian? Did he know about the Imperial arrest warrant? And if so, what would he do to them?

As they moved out of the bright courtyard into the dim temple it took a moment for his eyes to adjust. Then he saw a statue of a seated god in a huge semi-circular niche. The statue was made of black marble and the toga was made of some purple-red rock, perhaps porphyry. The eyes had been set with white and they looked almost alive.

'Lucius Domitius Pantera!' announced pink-eyed Albinus.

Juba gaped as the seated god rose up from its marble throne and moved forward.

This was no statue; it was his uncle, dressed in a scarlet toga.

He had an athlete's body and a perfectly proportioned head. Juba saw what his father might have been had he trained as an athlete.

'Greetings!' said their uncle, looking beyond them. 'Where are your parents? Are they not with you?' His voice was deep and his accent as cultured as any patrician in Rome.

'Uncle Pantera,' Juba sank to one knee and gestured to the others to do the same. 'Last month,' he said, 'some men came at midnight to confiscate our townhouse. Mater and Pater had to stay behind. They told us to come here. We humbly ask for salt and shelter. We have nowhere else to go.'

'Of course,' his uncle replied, as he helped Juba to his feet. 'You are most welcome here. Are you Fronto?'

'No, I am Juba. This is Fronto, my older brother.'

Pantera helped Fronto rise, clasped both shoulders and brought him close to kiss his forehead. Then he gave Juba a similar embrace. He pretended to start back upon seeing Ursula, who was bearing Meer the kitten on her left shoulder. 'You must be Ursula, the fierce little bear.' He gave her a dazzling smile.

156

Finally he turned to Bouda, standing straight and tall.

'And this lovely girl must be a native of the island,' he said. 'You have a look of the Iccni tribe? Perhaps you are descended from Queen Boudica?'

'How did you know that?' cried Fronto. 'Her name is Bouda. She's Boudica's great grand-daughter.'

'I'm sure she is,' Pantera said smoothly. He raised an eyebrow at Bouda.

Juba glanced at Bouda and frowned. She was gazing wide-eyed and open-mouthed at his uncle.

It was almost as if she recognised him.

Chapter Forty
TRICLINIUM

Juba had to wait over an hour to ask Bouda about his uncle. After their audience with Pantera, a slave boy had led them to the baths for a short session – the girls first and then the boys.

Coming out of the caldarium, Juba and Fronto had found fresh clothes laid out for them. Fronto put on a deep red synthesis, a special long tunic with a short cloak of the same colour attached. Juba's tunic was grey silk shot with green, a fabulously expensive fabric the same colour as his eyes. He guessed his uncle's slaves had been working hard to alter some of their master's garments.

The sun had just set and the sky was a pale lemon yellow.

As Juba and his brother followed another slave boy across the vast garden, he spotted Ursula and Bouda up ahead.

Running to catch up, Juba addressed Bouda in a low voice. 'Do you know my uncle from somewhere?'

'No,' she whispered back. She looked very pretty in a mint green cotton tunic over sky blue. 'I've never seen your uncle before. But he reminds me of someone.'

'Who?'

'Tyranus. The leader of the East End Gang.'

'Is Tyranus also from Africa?'

Bouda frowned. 'No. He is British. But he gives off the same scent of power, like an animal. Dangerous but exciting.' She gave her head a little shake. 'I can't describe it.'

'You described it very well,' Juba muttered.

The two blond slave boys trotted forward to show them to their places in the garden triclinium.

Their uncle was already there, reclining on the left-hand couch. A third slave stood at the foot of his couch; it was the boy who had urged Bouda to run away. Like the other two, he kept his head down.

As the slave boys removed their shoes, Loquax flew down from a grape arbour and settled on Ursula's shoulder. Juba and Fronto stretched out on the central couch, the girls on the right-hand one. As soon as they were settled, the three blond boys set food on the table before them. Then the slaves retreated to the open end of the triclinium and bowed their heads.

Suddenly, Juba realised something.

'Uncle Pantera,' he asked, 'why do you only have slaves with pale hair and blue eyes?'

His uncle lifted his hand as if to ask for silence. 'First things first,' he said. He lifted a silver pitcher of wine, poured a libation onto the ground and invoked the blessings of the gods. He handed the jug to the oldest boy so that he could serve them all. Only then did he turn to Juba.

'When I was about Ursula's age and living in Rome,' he said, 'I saw a rich patrician who had surrounded himself with black-skinned slaves. I never forgot that. I vowed that if I ever became rich that I would surround myself with white-skinned slaves. That is my type of justice.'

'But why have slaves at all?' Ursula said. 'Why can't we be free and work together?'

159

'Because, my dear, the world is not like that.' He took an olive from a bowl and then beckoned. One of the boys hurried forward with a shell-shaped silver bowl of scented water. Pantera rinsed his fingers in the water then wiped them on a napkin draped over the slave boy's arm. 'It is better to be an oppressor than one of the oppressed.'

Juba frowned. 'In book six of the *Aeneid*, Virgil says we Romans should spare the people we conquer.'

Uncle Pantera nodded. 'But in that same verse Anchises tells Aeneas to rule the nations by his power.'

'*Debellare superbos!*' quoted Fronto. 'Battle down the proud!'

Pantera nodded. 'Tell me, Juba: what are you trained for?'

The question took Juba by surprise.

'What do you mean?'

'What was your father's ambition for you?'

When Juba hesitated, Fronto raised his hand. '*I* was going to join the army,' he said. 'As an officer, of course.'

Pantera nodded at him and smiled. 'Excellent choice. And you, Juba?'

'Pater wanted me to climb the ladder of honours,' Juba said. 'His secretary taught us poetry and rhetoric.'

'So you can recite Virgil and a little Homer?'

'I can recite the whole *Aeneid*,' said Fronto.

'Excellent. And you, Juba?'

'Not as much as Fronto, but yes.'

His uncle held up his hand.

'But what can you *do*? Can you make a shoe out of leather? Can you spin a pot of clay, then bake it in a kiln? Can you beat red-hot iron into a blade or axe-head? Can you make enough garum to fill even a small jar?'

Juba shook his head. 'Those are jobs for the poorer classes.

160

Those of us who are rich have a responsibility to help the community. Pater used to take me to watch lawyers plead their cases. I like watching men fight for justice.'

Pantera smiled and shook his head. 'You speak of justice, but you just told me that being a cobbler, potter or blacksmith is for those lower than you. You think you are better just because your father had money. You think it is beneath you to work with your hands. Better let a poor man do it. Or a slave!'

'I can do things with my hands!' Juba said. 'I can scrub a ship's deck until it is as smooth as silk. I can drive a cart pulled by an ox, even one with hay on its horns. And I can mend a canvas sail with a bone needle and linen thread.'

His uncle snorted. 'And could you have done any of those things six weeks ago? Before you fled your childhood palace?'

'It wasn't a palace. It was just a big townhouse.'

'It was a palace. Full of slaves. Just like this one.'

'No!' Juba sat up on the dining couch. 'It wasn't like this. We treated our slaves well.' Even as he said it, he felt a pang of guilt as he remembered the cramped quarters off the storeroom, and how his personal slave Tutianus used to sleep on a rush mat on the cold floor of his bedroom, sometimes after warming Juba's bed. He recalled how he had beaten Tutianus twice, both times upon his father's orders.

'I treat my slaves well,' said his uncle. He gestured at the three barefoot blond boys in their cream tunics. 'They grew up in huts made of dung mixed with mud, sharing their living quarters with animals. Now they live here. Instead of whey and gruel, I give them wine and bread. And the ones I don't keep go to Italia, a land of grapes, olives and warm sunshine.'

'Maybe they like living with animals,' said Ursula. 'Maybe they prefer freedom to luxury.'

161

Juba frowned. 'What do you mean by *the ones you don't keep*? Where do you get these slaves from, anyway?'

'From slave-traders, of course.'

'Where do the slave-traders get them?'

'Most Britons are savages. They battle with each other and sell the captives.'

Juba's back twinged under his lowest right rib. Every time he felt it, it reminded him of the humiliation of being whipped.

'Your father and I are merchants,' said Pantera. 'He deals in hard, cold gems and I deal in living ones. At the beginning, he loaned me money. Later he came to disapprove of my trade. And yet he has slaves and he accepted them from me. He is a hypocrite!'

A thought struck Juba, one that made his flesh crawl. His personal slave Tutianus was fair-skinned and blond, like these boys. He had been a gift from Uncle Pantera on his visit five years previously.

'What's a hypocrite?' Ursula whispered.

'Someone who claims to be virtuous but really isn't,' Juba said miserably. 'Like me.'

Chapter Forty-One
PROCURATOR

At first, Fronto was happy.

It wasn't home, but it was the closest thing he could hope to find in this land so far from Rome.

Even the sky looked Roman: deep blue with bright stars. The slave boys lit bronze oil-lamps and the flames made the leaves of the arbour overhead glow like emeralds. There were linen cushions on the dining couches and silver cups for their wine.

But the food was too rich. Pantera's cook had prepared a patina like the one Bouda had bought in Londinium. There were also stuffed songbirds and a piglet with a plum in his mouth. A fish on a silver platter turned out to be made of chopped liver.

Fronto longed for the good but simple food his parents had served: black olives from Greece, hard-boiled eggs, cheese patina and roast chicken. Also, the mood was too stiff and formal; he missed the laughter of family meals.

Bouda, on the other hand, loved her first proper Roman banquet on a couch beneath a grape arbour. She kept smoothing the soft cotton of her mint green tunic and holding up her goblet to see the silver gleam in the lamplight.

'This is a wonderful palace,' she said. 'It must be worth a fortune.'

'You've only seen part of it,' said Uncle Pantera. 'Tomorrow I'll show you the game park.'

'Game park?' Fronto put down a half-nibbled songbird and looked at his uncle.

Pantera nodded. 'It's just south of the villa. I've stocked it with imported deer and even a bear. I'll take you boys hunting tomorrow.'

Fronto sat up straight. 'I love to hunt,' he said.

'Me, too,' Juba took a sip of his watered wine and then a deep breath. 'They say the governor owned this villa before you,' he ventured.

'Yes,' said Pantera, 'and a client king before that.'

'How did you get it from the governor?' he asked.

'It was a gift from the Emperor,' said Pantera.

Juba choked on his wine and Fronto wondered at his boldness.

Bouda was intrigued. 'Are you a friend of Domitian?' she asked.

'We have never met,' Pantera said, 'but I have done him many favours. I am hoping he will appoint me to be procurator of this province.'

'What does a procurator do?' Ursula asked. She was only eating bread sprinkled with garum.

'I know!' Fronto said. 'Serapion told me once. The procurator is the head tax collector, correct?'

Pantera raised an eyebrow. 'In very basic terms. He also oversees imperial estates and mines. It is an honoured position second in importance only to the governor.'

'Why not aim for the governorship?' Juba asked.

'The Emperor always appoints someone of the senatorial class to be governor of a province like Britannia,' said Pantera.

'Despite our great wealth, our family is of the equestrian class.'

'Serapion told us it's even better than being governor because you get more money and less responsibility,' said Fronto.

'He is quite correct.' Pantera almost purred.

'So you like this cold, wet province?' Juba asked.

'Yes,' said his uncle. 'Almost as much as Ursula loves it.'

Ursula looked up, startled. 'What makes you think I like Britannia?' she asked.

'Because you are of a choleric temperament, like me,' he said.

'What's choleric?' Bouda took a dainty bite of milk patina.

Pantera smiled at her. 'Those of us who are choleric have too much yellow bile. Our element is fire and our season is summer.'

He turned to Ursula, 'Your brothers have cool temperaments. Therefore, they like warmth. But you and I crave cool seasons and damp climates to balance our hot, dry humours.' He gestured at the star-studded sky, 'Admit it: you like it here in cool Britannia.'

Ursula shrugged. 'I like the animals. And the silver birch trees and the dawn chorus of birds and the green grass.'

'See?' her uncle said. 'Cool green grass is what those of a fiery nature crave.'

Bouda toyed with one of her copper ringlets. 'What temperament am I?' she asked.

But at that point a blond slave hurried up, bowed his head in respect and handed a small wax tablet to Pantera. Ursula's uncle angled it to catch the lamplight.

Ursula sat up eagerly. 'Is it news of our parents?'

'No,' her uncle replied. 'I have a visitor.' He turned to the boy. 'Take him to the blue tablinum and offer him refreshment. Tell him I will be there shortly.' He stood and brushed the crumbs from his scarlet synthesis. 'I must leave you. If I'm not back by the time you finish eating, the boys will show you to your sleeping quarters. I have provided the finest feather mattresses for each of you.' He smiled at Ursula. 'Even those of you with a fiery temperament appreciate a warm bed. And those of you who appreciate luxury,' Juba saw him turn his jet-black eyes on Bouda, 'will love it.'

Chapter Forty-Two
CATENAE

'Meer! Where are you?' whispered Ursula later that night. '*Hic, hic, hic!*'

After dinner, slave boys had showed the four of them to a pair of rooms in the south wing, not far from the baths. Black and red painted walls for the boys, a green garden painting for the girls. But sometime in the night, long after the slaves extinguished all but one of the oil-lamps, Ursula woke to find Meer gone.

Despite her uncle's promise, she found the feather bed too soft. She got up and, wearing only her new cinnamon-coloured linen undertunic, tiptoed over to see if her kitten was with Bouda.

'Meer?' she whispered again. '*Hic, hic, hic!*' In the eerie light of a nearly full moon, the brick walkway seemed as red as blood. The moon-shadows cast by the columns were pitch black.

Creeping from one column's shadow to the next, Ursula was reminded of the night they had fled their Roman townhouse. Had it been not quite two months ago? It seemed like a year.

Surely two months was long enough for her parents to escape the Emperor and come to them? The thought made her feel sick so she pushed it away and concentrated on finding Meer.

If I were a kitten, where would I go?

She got down on hands and knees. It was scary to be so low. The columns loomed above her and the shadows they cast were inky black. The brick walkway was blood red, but at least it was not slippery marble.

She cupped her ears, but the villa was silent.

Then she sniffed the air and caught a sudden whiff of fermented salty fish. Garum! She could smell garum. She sniffed her fingertips but the smell wasn't there. On hands and knees, and sniffing with her nose, Ursula followed the scent along the walkway, moving from red brick to black shadow and back again.

She was just about to get up when she heard Meer's distinctive '*Meeer!*' coming from a doorway on her left.

She crawled to the doorway and peeped in. A single burning oil-lamp on a table showed her a small, empty anteroom. On the table was an iron key and on the floor nearby was a tray with a dozen spoons in as many empty bowls. She could smell barley porridge. But no fish-sauce.

The dark rectangle of a doorway gaped opposite and she heard another miaow from the inner room.

There was no decoration on the walls and the floor was concrete. These were probably the slave quarters. There was no chance of encountering her uncle in here, so she stood up, brushed the dust from her knees and took the clay oil-lamp from the table.

'Meer?' she whispered. 'Meer are you in there?'

'*Meeer!*' She saw her kitten's golden eyes reflecting in the darkness.

Ursula extended the oil-lamp and as it shed its light she nearly screamed.

Surrounding Meer were a dozen pairs of blue eyes gazing

back at her. She stepped into the room and gaped: some children about her age were clustered around three little girls who were stroking Meer. Their clothes were grubby but she could see they had once been fine garments in chequered patterns of blue, yellow and green. As they moved, she heard the metallic clink of chains.

Lifting her oil-lamp and moving closer, she saw that they were chained to one another at their necks and then to a ring in the wall. All but one of them was fair-haired and blue-eyed. The youngest of them was a little boy with brown eyes and dusky skin like hers.

'Audax?' she whispered.

The toddler eagerly lifted his head and she saw the spark of hope gleam in his eyes and then die.

The look of bleak resignation on his face almost broke her heart.

'Who are you?' Ursula asked the children. 'Where are you from?'

'We come from our village,' said one boy. 'All except for him. How did you know his name?'

'His mama is looking for him.'

'Is my mama looking for me?' asked a girl.

They were all talking now and she couldn't understand. Finally the oldest boy shushed them. They seemed to accept him as their leader for they all grew quiet. He turned to Ursula.

'Are you the Dark One's daughter?' he asked. 'Will he let us go home?'

With a shiver of horror Ursula realised they were captive British children.

And her uncle was selling them as slaves.

Chapter Forty-Three
CLAVIS

'All twelve of the British children are freeborn,' Bouda told Juba half hour later. 'And that one,' she pointed, 'must be the little boy you've been looking for. He was brought here just over a week ago. The rest have been here for ten days.'

They were all in the smelly room full of chained children. Ursula had woken them and quietly led them here.

'Ask them what happened,' Juba asked. 'And where they're from.'

Bouda spoke rapidly and the oldest boy answered. Juba only understood half of the words he used; it was good to have a translator.

Bouda looked at him. 'The boy calls himself Sulinus. He says they're of the Belgae tribe from a village near Aquae Sulis. That's a famous sanctuary with healing waters about a week's walk northwest of here. He says three men of the Durotriges tribe captured them when they were coming back to their village from a festival last month.'

Juba shook his head in confusion. 'What are they doing here? Why are they chained up like slaves?'

'Don't you see?' Ursula cried. 'Uncle Pantera bought them from the slave-traders and he's going to sell them in Rome!'

Juba felt sick as Bouda nodded. 'This boy says the Dark One bought them from the Durotrigan raiders. The tribes used to steal cattle from each other,' she added. 'Now they take children. He says the Dark One told them they are going on a ship to a faraway land where they will be happy.'

Fronto nodded. 'One of the ships we saw this afternoon.'

'And if he takes them from his own private harbour,' said Juba, 'he doesn't have to pay export tax.'

Bouda spoke to the oldest boy again, in fluent Brittonic.

This time, Juba knew enough to understand the boy's answer. He recognized the words for *Yes, Durotriges, Ship* and *Faraway*. 'The Dark One is our uncle, isn't he?' he said. 'Does he know about this?'

'Yes,' Bouda said. 'They say he watched while the White One put on their chains.'

'But they're freeborn,' cried Ursula. 'How could he do that?'

'Ask him about Audax,' Juba said.

This time he understood perfectly as Bouda asked. 'Where did the little boy come from?'

'We don't know,' Sulinus said. 'The White One brought him in a few days ago. He keeps asking for Mama and also someone called Ubi.'

'Nubia is his mother's name!' Ursula remembered.

Juba felt the anger rise into his cheeks. He held the oil-lamp closer to the iron ring around a little girl's neck. The skin was red and sore.

'We should take them to the baths!' Ursula cried. 'And feed them.'

Juba shook his head. 'That won't help,' he said. 'Uncle Pantera is just going to ship them to Rome and sell them.'

171

'We can't let him do that!' Ursula said. 'We have to set them free.'

'But they're his property,' Fronto said, tapping the floor. 'He paid for them. Correct?' He looked at Bouda.

'Yes, that boy says he gave gold to their kidnappers.'

'Uncle Pantera had no right to buy them,' Juba muttered.

'We have slaves,' Fronto pointed out.

Juba shook his head. 'They were home grown, not freeborn.' But he thought again of Tutianus, a gift from his uncle.

'They must be scared,' Ursula turned to Bouda. 'What's that little girl asking you? She keeps tugging your tunic.'

Bouda laughed. 'She wants to know how to train a kitten to go onto your shoulder. Most cats she knows do what they like and never ride on people.'

'Tell her we were on a ship for over a month when my kitten was tiny. She had to learn to cling tight so she wouldn't get washed overboard.'

The little girl said something and Bouda's smile faded. She turned to Juba. 'She wants to know if she can she have a kitten for their sea voyage. They're all going on a boat tomorrow.'

'How does she know they're sailing tomorrow?'

'We heard some slaves talking,' said Sulinus.

'Juba!' Ursula's eyes filled with tears. 'We have to set them free!'

Juba stared at the faint lamplight. *Father Jupiter, what should I do?*

He pressed his fingertips to his scalp, trying to calm his swirl of thoughts.

Ursula held up an iron key.

'Juba, we have to do this!' she whispered.

'We can't!' gasped Bouda. 'What would your uncle say?'

'Uncle Pantera will be very angry with us,' Fronto said. 'He'll be very angry, very angry, very angry.'

Juba looked up sharply. His brother was using the little statue of Jupiter to tap the door frame obsessively: *right, left, right.*

'Don't be upset,' Ursula patted Fronto's back. 'When Pater and Mater get here they'll explain it to him. They'll defend us.'

Juba felt sick.

Their parents were never coming. Uncle Pantera was their only chance of a home.

Bouda said it clearly. 'Juba, if you take these children back to their home then you'll make an enemy of your own uncle.'

'I know.'

Juba took a deep breath. The time had come to tell his brother and sister the truth.

'Ursula, Fronto,' he said. 'I'm afraid we will never see Mater and Pater again. If we take these children home we will lose any chance we ever had of living here.'

'Don't say that!' cried Ursula. 'Don't say that!'

And Fronto was now tapping more urgently than ever, repeating over and over: 'I did it wrong. I did it wrong.'

'Fronto,' Juba said. 'Remember Aeneas fleeing burning Troy. He had to leave his wife behind. But it was the will of the gods. He had a destiny. Remember?'

Fronto nodded.

'So tell me,' said Juba. 'What would Aeneas do?'

'Aeneas would do what is right and just in the eyes of the gods.' Fronto replied mechanically, but Juba saw that he had stopped tapping.

And he knew what he had to do.

Chapter Forty-Four
DAMA

It did not take them long to find a way out of the palace.
Juba remembered that the hot baths had to be heated by a furnace and that these usually had access in an outside wall. Sure enough, they found their exit in a room between the latrine and the caldarium. It was a storeroom with rags, twig-brooms and wooden buckets. At its back was a wooden door with a big bar on the inside to prevent those outside from coming in. But nothing stopped them from going out.

The moon was still up and it showed a wall stretching south, with trees behind it. He could hear an owl hooting.

'That must be the game park,' he whispered to the others.

On his left, to the southeast, was the inlet with the two ships. One of them was to take the children away the next morning.

They needed to get to the main road, but it was to the north, on the far side. If they went directly there, they would have to pass the front of the villa and the guards might raise the alarm. They couldn't go east because of the water.

Behind him he heard Fronto nervously tap the wall of the villa. 'Shhh!' he hissed. 'Listen! We're going to follow the wall south, skirt the bottom of the park and then, when we've put some distance between us and the palace, we'll head back up to the main road. From there we'll try to get a lift to Aquae Sulis so that we can return you to your families.'

A small hot hand grasped his. He looked down and saw little Audax.

'Are you coming with me?' he whispered.

Audax nodded solemnly.

Holding the toddler's hand, Juba started along the path that ran beside the villa. He crouched down so that nobody glancing out of their window would see his head moving past. The other children followed his lead.

Soon they were able to stand upright, for they had left the buildings of the palace behind and were skirting the east wall of the game park.

After nearly a tenth of an hour Juba noticed the path becoming soggier. He carried on, expecting the wall to turn at its southern border. But instead of turning, the wall ended.

Juba frowned. If this was a game park with deer, hare, badgers and bear, where was the southern boundary?

Little Audax slipped and would have plunged into a deep channel if he hadn't been holding Juba's hand. Juba pulled him back onto the boggy ground and took a step back.

'Careful!' he whispered to the children behind him. 'There's a ditch! I almost fell in.'

Now he could see the deep channel, so straight that it must be man-made, and he could hear water gurgling.

He turned his little band west, towards the setting moon.

Audax tugged at his hand. 'Lift,' he said.

'Just a little longer,' Juba promised.

'Lift,' repeated Audax.

Juba sighed and picked him up. A low mist blanketed the marshy area and it was hard to see where he was stepping.

Behind him some of the children were whimpering. They had been captive for ten days, walked a hundred miles and eaten only a few bowls of porridge. They were cold, damp, hungry and homesick.

It was Fronto who came up with an idea to lift their spirits.

He began to chant a version of the marching song the auxiliaries had sung, one simple enough for the British children to learn.

'*Right, left, right,*' he chanted. '*Right, left, right!*
'*Dextra, sinister, dextra, sinister!*
'*sin, dex, sin . . . sin, dex, sin!*'

The children picked it up easily and were soon chanting happily. But when Juba heard some ducks quacking far out on the water to his left, it occurred to him that sound carried in this flat silent world. Reluctantly, he told the children to whisper.

He had just adjusted his grip on Audax when a girl's shrill scream pierced the air.

At that moment, a dark shape came galloping past, so close that it almost knocked him over. Only after it was gone did he realise it had been a deer. Not a small deer but a great stag with antlers.

His whole body went cold as he remembered his uncle had mentioned having a bear as well as deer in the park.

'Shhh!' he whispered over his shoulder. 'Quiet as mice now!'

He hoisted Audax into a piggyback position.

The mist was becoming thicker and the ground was getting soggier. Audax's chubby arms were tight round his neck. Juba remembered carrying Fronto when they had fled Rome. He set his jaw and carried on.

Then, just when he thought things could not get worse, Juba realised that water was lapping around his feet.

'I've read about this,' Fronto's voice came from behind him. 'There are places on the coast of Gaul where the seawater goes out and comes in twice a day. They're called tides. We don't have them in Italia because the sea is enclosed, but Oceanus has no borders.'

'Are tides dangerous?' Juba asked him.

'Yes,' Fronto said. 'We should go north right away.'

Juba nodded miserably.

If they turned north before they reached the western wall they would be trapped in his uncle's game park with wild animals.

But if they kept going west they might be drowned by the incoming tide.

He thought he had been leading the kidnapped children home but it seemed he was taking them back to captivity. Or to their deaths.

Chapter Forty-Five
HORREUM

It was little Audax who saw it first.

'Lift!' he said, pointing with his chubby finger. Juba squinted. Looming out of the fog up ahead was a rectangular wooden building on stilts.

'Look!' Ursula whispered. 'But what is it?'

'It looks like an army storehouse,' Fronto said. 'They build them on stilts so mice can't get at the grain. I wonder if there's a fort here?' he peered into the tatters of fog.

'There was a fort a long time ago,' said a child's voice. 'Before the palace was built.'

Juba whirled around. 'Who said that?'

'Me, sir. My name is Toutis.' A blond boy emerged and looked up at Juba. The huge setting moon showed his clean hair and tunic of fine, unbleached linen.

'You're not one of the kidnapped children!' Juba cried. 'You're one of my uncle's slaves! You're the one who told Bouda to run away.'

The boy called Toutis nodded. 'Your uncle bought me from kidnappers, two summers ago.'

Juba stopped in his tracks. 'My uncle's been buying kidnapped children for two years?' he said.

Toutis nodded again. 'He sends most to Rome, but he sometimes keeps one or two for himself.'

Juba shook his head to try to clear it. So many different thoughts were tangled there, like coloured strands in a wool basket. He needed to focus on the most important one: keeping the children alive until he could return them to their parents. His mother's words came back. *Save the children.*

'Is the storehouse safe?' he asked. 'Can we hide there?'

'I don't know, sir. All I know is that the water comes in and out twice a day. And the older slaves say there was a fort here once when the ground was drier.'

'There must be a way to get in,' Juba muttered. 'Maybe round the other side.'

'Lift,' said Audax pointing.

Juba nodded. 'Yes,' he said. 'We're going there. By the gods, you're heavy!'

He turned to Fronto, to ask if he could carry Audax for a while. But Fronto was already carrying the youngest girl. Her thumb was in her mouth and she was asleep on his chest. Juba gave his brother a rueful grin, shifted Audax to his left side and started for the storehouse.

Soon the water was up to his ankles and the fog was up to his waist. Some of the younger children were nearly hidden by it. 'Hang on to the cloak or tunic of the person in front of you!' Juba whispered over his shoulder as he shifted Audax back to his right side.

The storehouse seemed bigger and darker the closer they came, but Juba sent up an arrow prayer of thanks to the gods when he saw narrow steps leading up. 'Wait here,' he said to the others. 'I'll go first and make sure it's safe.'

But little Audax was already reaching for the stairs. He

caught one of the upper steps, writhed out of Juba's tired arms and scrambled up like a monkey.

Juba followed, cursing as his foot went through the rotten wood of the third step. But he righted himself and tested the other six steps before going in.

'Come on, Ursula. Watch out for that step.'

Ursula nodded grimly. Meer was mewing on her shoulder. When she was at eye level, Juba stopped her. 'Where's Loquax?' he asked.

'I had to leave him behind,' she said. 'I forgot to put him in his cage after dinner and I couldn't risk calling to him.'

Before he could comfort her, she carried on up the steps. As the last of the children came inside they discovered that Loquax was not the only one left behind.

'Where's Bouda?' called Fronto from the bottom of the stairs. 'She's not here.' He was staring back towards the east, in the direction they had just come.

Juba's stomach flipped like a dying fish.

He realised he had not seen her once since they left the palace. 'Has anyone seen Bouda?' he asked, his voice sounding strange in the boxlike space.

It was dark; only a few shafts of silver moonlight illuminated the shivering children. There was no sign of Bouda.

'Come up, big brother,' Juba said. 'She'll be all right. She's good at surviving. We'll find her when the sun comes up and the tide goes down.'

Fronto came up the steps in silence and did not even tap the door frame as he entered.

'She didn't come with us,' said Toutis the slave boy.

Juba looked at him. 'What?'

'When I went out of the palace to follow you, I saw her going back to her bedroom.'

Juba's shoulders slumped. Bouda had made it perfectly clear that she preferred luxury to justice, but it was still like a punch in his gut.

'Bouda stayed behind?' It was his sister's voice.

'Yes,' said Juba miserably. 'She's probably fast asleep in her warm feather bed.'

Chapter Forty-Six
TENEBRAE

J uba could hear children whimpering.

His teeth were chattering, with dread as much as with cold.

'What have I done?' he whispered to himself.

The answer came in his head: *You brought half-starved children out into a dark, wet, dangerous night and gave them false hope.*

'You did a brave thing,' said Toutis's voice close to his ear. 'I wanted to help the children run away but I was too scared.'

'How old are you?'

'Eight,' said Toutis. 'I think.'

Juba peered through the darkness at him. The boy was barefoot, and wearing only an unbelted linen tunic

'Here,' Juba offered. 'Put my cloak around you. You must be freezing.'

'No. You need it.'

'Then come under with me,' Juba lifted up part of the cloak and felt the boy's skinny body nestle close. *By the gods, he was cold!*

'Everybody,' Juba said. 'Huddle together for warmth. Ursula, you take some girls under your cloak.'

'I already have,' came her voice.

'Fronto—'

'I have, too.'

'Who's left?' Juba asked in halting Brittonic.

'Me!'

'Me!'

'Me!'

'Come on, then,' Juba grunted.

They came to him like puppies, squeezing their little bodies under his cloak, pushing and nudging him with their cold hard heads. He didn't know whether to laugh or cry.

Presently, he was wavering between a light sleep and drowsy wakefulness.

At one point he must have been dreaming, because he saw his mother coming towards him out of the darkness.

She was smiling and holding his father's tawny woollen cloak in her hands. As she drew closer, he noticed drops of red blood on the cloak. Even as he watched, more drops appeared in the tawny wool, spreading and growing, growing and spreading. Soon the cloak was no longer the colour of a heroic lionskin, but a vivid blood-red.

His smiling mother tried to put the sodden, steaming garment on him, but he cried out in horror, and pushed it away.

He burst out of sleep, gasping like a swimmer coming up for air. The world around him was as black with his eyes open as it had been with them closed.

A wave of despair washed over him.

A soft voice came out of the darkness. 'Juba?' It was his sister Ursula.

'Yes?' he whispered.

'Are you all right? You cried out for Mater in your sleep.'

'Yes,' he lied. 'I'm fine.'

Her voice came again. 'Mater and Pater are dead, aren't they? That's why they're not coming.'

He swallowed. He had never said it out loud. He knew when he did, it would somehow make it real.

'Yes,' he said at last. 'They died in Rome. I saw them when I went back for our household gods.'

'Are you sure?' That was Fronto.

The storehouse was so dark and the memory so vivid that Juba might have been standing by the porter's screen back in Rome. If he looked behind it, he would see his parents lying on the porter's couch to one side of the vestibule.

'When I found them,' he said, 'they were lying in each other's arms. They look very peaceful, as if they were sleeping. I could smell something bittersweet. I think they took hemlock.'

'What's hemlock?'

'It's a kind of plant that puts you to sleep forever.'

'Like poison?'

'Yes, but it doesn't hurt.'

There was a long pause, then Ursula's small voice. 'Why didn't they just run away?'

'Because Domitian's men would have caught them. They knew they couldn't betray us if they were dead. They gave their lives to save ours.'

'Oh Juba!' He could hear her soft sobs and also the consoling murmurs of the four little girls snuggling up to her.

Fronto was muttering

'Fronto?' Juba whispered. 'Are you in one of your trances?'

'No,' Fronto said. 'I can't get revenge if I'm in a trance.'

Juba opened his mouth, then closed it again.

'Your cloak is bumpy,' said Toutis to Juba as he shifted on the wooden floor.

'I know,' Juba said. 'I don't know how my father endured it. But it's a good warm cloak, isn't it?'

He felt the little slave boy nod. 'My mother used to sew coins into the seams of my father's cloak,' Toutis said. 'For emergencies.'

'That's a good idea.' Juba looked down at Toutis. He could see the pale oval of the boy's face.

'Look, Juba!' Ursula whispered. 'It's getting light.'

He undid the toggle of his cloak and spread it over the five boys who had been clinging to him. He left the warmth reluctantly, crawling on his hands and knees towards the storehouse door.

'Pollux!' he cursed softly, as a splinter pierced the palm of his hand.

When he reached the open doorway, he could still see a few fading stars in the sky. He realised he was looking north. A dawn breeze blew the last tatters of ground mist and brought a whiff of fish sauce.

'Why do I smell garum?' he muttered.

'It's a secret fish-pickle factory.' Toutis had come to join him. The dim light showed his arm pointing west.

'A garum factory?'

The boy nodded.

It was growing lighter by the minute. Juba could see the marshes, with patches of water reflecting a rosy glow towards the east.

'Is the tide going out?' he asked. 'Already?'

'Yes,' said Toutis. 'It comes in twice a day and then goes out twice a day. I think it is still going out.'

Juba peered into the west. All he could see were dark clumps of marsh against patches of reflecting water. His nostrils flared with the scent of salty seawater, damp reeds and mud.

Toutis tugged Juba's tunic. 'Oxcarts full of salt arrive from the salt pans near here every Saturn's Day morning and go back empty,' he whispered. 'Garum needs lots of salt and we don't have enough at Fishbrook.'

Juba glanced back towards the children huddling against the black walls of the storehouse. 'The carts go back empty?' he whispered.

Toutis nodded.

'But don't the salt gatherers work for my uncle?'

'Yes, but they live further west, and the man who drives the cart hates him.'

'How do you know that?'

'House-slaves know everything. The man in charge is called Fortunatus. He told us. '

Juba squinted, trying to see some sign of the factory. 'How long will it take us to walk there?'

'Not long. But the tide will start coming in again soon.'

Juba nodded, then clapped his hands for attention and turned to give the children the news. But what he saw made him falter.

The sun had risen and its beams pierced through cracks and knotholes in the aging wood planks. The rays looked like a blood red arrows.

Without thinking, Juba made the sign against evil. He was sure it was a message from the gods. But what did it mean?

He would find out soon.

Chapter Forty-Seven
PALUS

Ursula followed Juba across the boggy marsh. The sun was up, growing stronger and warmer as it rose. Soon her damp clothes began to steam along with the mud and reeds. She had given the last of the milk in her wineskin to Meer; it was only a mouthful. Her kitten purred softly in her ear.

Brown birds perched on the marsh grasses. Some chittered urgently and others sang sweet refrains in their own metre. It was as if they were trying to tell her something.

'Sedge Warblers scold,' she heard Toutis say. 'And Reed Warblers encourage. Look! The Reed Warblers were right!'

Toutis was pointing to a freshwater brook, hardly more than a rivulet, which sparkled in the morning sunshine.

With squeals of delight, the children fell to their stomachs and drank greedily, some lapping like Meer the kitten. The water was sweet and cold, and Ursula heard Juba whisper a thank you to the Genius of the Brook. He thanked Sol Invictus, too: the Unconquered Sun, who had driven away the bleak night and brought light, warmth and birdsong.

Ursula thanked them too, and also Venus, safely nestled next to her rabbit-fur puppy.

When they rose, they found the fronts of their tunics were

muddy and soaked. The littlest girl, Velvinna, started crying. Ursula comforted her by letting her hold Canicula, her rabbit fur puppy.

The ground was getting waterlogged, so Fronto invented a game. You had to avoid the sucking mud by using hummocks of marsh grass as stepping stones.

Some of the jumps were too big for Velvinna. Ursula caught her hand and helped her leap from one to the next.

'What's that?' Velvinna pointed to the low, white-plastered wall visible above marsh grasses.

Ursula crouched beside her. 'I think that's where they make . . .' She paused, and not knowing the British word for fish-pickle sauce, finally used the Latin words: 'Garum. Liquamen. Allec.'

The little girl nodded. 'Stinky Roman juice,' she said, and wrinkled her nose.

Ursula laughed. 'Yes. Stinky Roman juice. I don't eat animal meat, but I love garum. Come on: jump!'

She was suddenly aware that even the hummocks were becoming soggy. Glancing south, she saw that half the marsh was liquid gold in the early light. The tide was coming in fast.

'Juba!' she cried.

'I know.' His voice was grim.

They reached the factory just in time. Its outer wall was about Ursula's height, and built on a slightly raised bank of land, with a footpath running round its base. Juba and Fronto were helping the children up the small bank onto the dry path. Holding Velvinna's hand, Ursula ran up, too, and then grabbed the top of the wall to stop herself from falling back. Cautiously, she stood on tiptoe and peeped to see what was on the other side.

The smell was almost overpowering. Pulling up the neck

of her tunic to cover her nose, she looked into a large open courtyard with a small plaster-covered shed in one corner. In the centre of the courtyard were various tanks and pools, open to the sky. Nearest to her was a large rectangular tank and beyond it four smaller square pools. They all had low raised walls around them, about a foot high. The biggest tank reminded her of the open-air swimming pool in Rome's most luxurious baths. But instead of clear water, it contained a stinking brown mixture of anchovy guts, mackerel blood and salt. The four smaller tanks on the far side of the big one were not unlike the warm plunge in her family's bath annex. They were filled with brown liquid in varying tints. There were also big pitch-lined baskets draped with sheets of linen cloth that acted as strainers.

'I want to look, too!' whispered Velvinna, clutching the rabbit puppy in one hand.

Ursula lifted her up and glanced around.

To her left was the sea. To her right, perhaps half a mile to the north, was a line of tall poplar trees.

'Is that the road to Noviomagus?' she heard Juba ask.

'Yes, I think so,' said Toutis. 'I haven't been outside the palace since they first caught me.'

'Where are the factory slaves?' Juba asked.

Toutis frowned. 'Fortunatus says the sun and the salt do the work. There's just a slave boy who opens the doors to let in the weekly delivery.'

Juba frowned. 'Then where's the slave boy?'

'Water!' said Velvinna, pointing down.

Ursula looked down. The tide had come in and they were now on an island surrounded by water.

'Lift!' said Audax, stretching his chubby arms up to Juba.

'Good idea' cried Juba. 'I think we'd better go over the wall.'

But before they could move any closer, they heard a deep barking from inside.

'Dog!' said Audax, excited.

'That's why they don't have a guard,' breathed Ursula. 'They have a dog. Can you see it?' she asked her brother.

'No,' said Juba.

'Me neither,' said Fronto.

Ursula looked down. The water was lapping at their feet. 'I'm good with animals,' she said. 'Let me go in first. Does anybody have food? Anything at all?'

Fronto reached into the neck of his tunic and pulled out a honey and almond pastry. 'It's my last one,' he said sheepishly. 'From dinner. But you can have it.'

'Shall I look after Meer?' Juba asked.

Ursula handed him her kitten. 'If anything happens to me,' she said in a trembling voice, 'please take care of her.'

Chapter Forty-Eight
CANIS

'Are you sure you want to go down there?' Juba asked his sister.

Ursula nodded. 'The dog's probably locked up or on a chain,' she said. 'He'd come closer if he could.'

'Good thinking,' said Juba, but he could feel her trembling as he helped her over. She hung for a moment on the inside, then landed lightly.

'Lift!' said Audax. Juba lifted the toddler and they watched Ursula walk in the direction of the barking.

'Doggie!' said Audax.

Ursula disappeared behind the square shed and the barking got more frenzied.

But a moment later, the barking stopped and Ursula soon re-appeared. 'I was right,' she said. 'He's chained up. And he likes pastries!'

'Any sign of the slave boy?'

She shook her head.

Juba turned to his brother. 'Help me over the wall, Fronto, and then hand down the children.'

Fronto nodded. He laced his fingers together, making a step for Juba to stand on.

'Sorry,' Juba muttered as he put his muddy boot into Fronto's hands. A heartbeat later he was over the wall.

The drop on the other side was not too great. Juba held out his arms for little Audax. Some of the bigger children could jump down by themselves.

Last of all came his brother.

'Just in time!' panted Fronto, as he landed inside the wall. 'My boots were starting to fill up with water.' He sat down to pull them off and empty them.

Juba turned. The children were staring into the tanks of fermenting fish guts in fascination. Some were holding their noses. Others were watching Meer, who was crouched at the edge of a tank, happily lapping at the fish-sauce. Three of the older boys hurried after Audax who had run to investigate the dog. Juba could see him now, a huge black mastiff. Toutis was holding the back of Audax's tunic to keep him out of range of the foam-flecked jaws.

'I'm hungry,' whimpered Velvinna.

Juba went to the storeroom door and gave it a push.

'I tried that already,' said Ursula. 'It's locked.'

'That's strange,' Juba said.

Fronto went to the storeroom door and touched the sides: *right, left, right.* 'It can't hurt,' he smiled.

'Come on,' Juba beckoned. 'Let's stand in the warm sun behind the shed. We can dry off while we're waiting for the salt delivery. Then we'll try to get a ride to Noviomagus. From there we can go to Aquae Sulis.'

The children dutifully followed him and sat with their backs against the plaster wall, near a dozen amphorae.

Fronto examined one of the amphorae. 'These are fakes!' he said suddenly.

'What? How can it be fake?' Juba frowned at them. The amphorae were shaped like fat carrots. Their pointy bottoms ended in distinctive blobs, exactly like the ones he and Fronto had brought up the gangplank at Baia Claudia.

'Touch it,' said Fronto. 'The clay is different.'

Juba reached out and touched one. It was smooth and slightly chalky under his fingertips. He remembered the rough texture of the real Spanish amphorae he had helped carry onto the *Centaur*.

'This clay is smoother,' he said.

Fronto nodded. 'The Spanish ones are rougher, but you wouldn't know from looking at them. Even the colour is the same. You'd only know if you handled the real ones, or carried them, as we have.'

'By all the gods!' Juba said. 'I know why our uncle is so rich. He doesn't import his garum from Spain. He makes it here in Britannia and then puts it in amphorae exactly like the Spanish ones. He just pretends that his garum comes from Spain!'

'Why would he do that?' Fronto said.

'Because people pay more for fancy imported garum,' Juba said. 'Far more.'

'But to sell garum from Britannia and pretend it's from Spain is cheating,' Ursula said.

Juba nodded grimly. 'It looks as if our uncle did not get rich by noble means.'

'Nor did your father,' said a familiar accented voice behind him.

Juba scrambled to his feet as a man in a cloak emerged from the open door of the storeroom. He was middle-aged with a mop of dark hair, olive skin and a fine profile. Juba could smell the distinctive turpentine smell of his perfume.

'Serapion!' cried Fronto.

Juba felt a surge of delight at the sight of a familiar face. Then he cocked his head in puzzlement. 'How did you find us?'

His tutor scowled. 'At great expense. Travelling on leaky riverboats and staying in bedbug-infested taverns. I have now exhausted the meagre savings I earned serving your father. You'd better make this worth my while.'

Juba was confused. 'What are you talking about?'

Behind Serapion, Ursula was silently saying something to Juba. She was pointing at the back of Serapion's cloak and making a roof over her head with her hands.

'I have made a long and dangerous journey,' Serapion glowered. 'And I would hate it to be in vain.'

Understanding drenched Juba like a bucket of cold water.

'You're the delator!' Juba said. 'The one who told the Emperor we were traitors. You're the man in the hooded cloak who rode with the soldiers in Ostia. How did you find us?'

'Where else could you go but to your only living relative?' he sneered. 'As I said, I made my way across Gaul and arrived at your uncle's villa last night. I was going to have an audience with him this morning but last night I met someone who told me that you had run away. Later I heard chanting drifting across the marshes. At first light we left the villa and walked in the direction from which the chanting had come. I saw this was the only place where you could shelter from the incoming tide. A helpful young slave let me in.'

He gestured towards dark shadows at the back of the storeroom and a boy in an unbelted linen tunic emerged. There was something wrong with his legs, but Juba couldn't tell what.

'And this young lady,' Serapion gestured again, 'is the one who told me you had run away.'

Juba felt sick as the second figure emerged from the storeroom into the bright morning light.

'Bouda?'

'I'm sorry!' she whispered, her face as white as chalk.

Serapion pulled a dagger from his belt. 'At long last,' he said. 'I can finish the task I started two months ago.'

Chapter Forty-Nine
GARUM

Serapion stepped forward. 'Where are they?' His tone was pleasant but his smile was ice.

Juba tried to back away, but the children had scurried to hide behind his cloak and they blocked his retreat. The others cowered behind Fronto and Ursula.

'Where are who?' Juba asked, his throat dry.

His tutor's icy smile faded. 'Don't play stupid. Where is the treasure?'

'What treasure?' Juba said. 'The Emperor confiscated everything!'

'Not quite everything,' Serapion said coldly. 'Your father sold his most valuable furniture, sculptures and tapestries while I was in Naples. I returned to find the house half empty. He must have made a fortune. And what is the easiest way to carry a fortune?'

'Gems and precious stones,' Juba replied. 'But all Pater's gems were gone. I looked in the box. It was empty.'

'Your father taught you well.' Serapion examined the sharp edge of his dagger. 'You are an excellent liar.'

'I'm not lying!' cried Juba. 'Pater's gem box was empty!'

'Because he gave them to you!' snarled Serapion, pointing his weapon at Juba.

'I only got one of the gems,' Juba said. 'Mater's Minerva cameo. And robbers stole that from me.'

Still brandishing the dagger in his right hand, Serapion used his left hand to fish in the neck of his tunic. 'Oh, yes,' he said, pulling out the Minerva cameo. 'I have that, but even at the point of death the robbers swore that was the only gem they took from you.'

'You killed the robbers?' Juba felt dizzy.

'And I will kill you, too,' said Serapion. 'If you don't tell me where the other jewels are. I would be satisfied with the Pearl of Iris.'

'I don't know!' cried Juba. 'I swear I don't know.'

And then a revelation struck him like Jupiter's bolt.

All this time the gems had been with him.

He had been fabulously rich, but he hadn't realised it.

Back in Rome, he could have bought a dozen wet nurses for baby Dora. He could have bought a merchant ship of their own in Ostia. He could have purchased a carruca with a yoke of snow-white oxen to pull it. He could have gilded their horns, and still had money left over.

Serapion had been watching him closely. He laughed. 'You didn't even know. How stupid can you be?'

Juba nodded. He felt sick. But also furious at Serapion. The Stoics taught that anger was a bad emotion, but he knew in this case it would give him strength. He let it flow through him.

'You betrayed my father,' he said. 'You're the one who told Domitian about his wealth. He always rewards informers. What was he going to give you?'

'He promised me your townhouse,' said Serapion, 'and he was going to keep the gems. This one of course,' he fingered the Minerva cameo, 'but also the Pearl of Iris. I can't go back without it.'

He grabbed Ursula and pressed the knife to her throat.

'Tell me where the jewels are, Lucius Domitius Juba, or I'll kill your family and friends, starting with this one.'

Juba's anger melted like snow. What could he do?

Ursula screamed and kicked, and Serapion struggled to hold her still.

Suddenly, a small grey blur moved away from the biggest fish tank and scampered up Ursula's pine green cloak. It was her kitten, Meer, trained to obey her mistress's warning cry.

With a hiss, she leapt at Serapion's face and scrabbled with her needle sharp claws.

Serapion yelped in surprise and dropped the knife. As he flailed to keep his balance, Ursula brought her elbow sharply into his stomach.

'Ooof!' Serapion grunted.

He was on his hands and knees at the side of the pool.

Before Juba could react, Fronto ran forward and kicked his former tutor hard.

Serapion fell back into the pool of fish guts, splashing garum everywhere. The children squealed and clapped.

But Juba knew they had only bought themselves a few moments.

Chapter Fifty
CINGULUM

'Come on!' cried Juba, as Serapion splashed and gasped in the pool of garum. 'Before he gets out!'

He tried to run but the lame boy threw himself to the ground and clung to Juba's ankles.

'Tie me up,' the boy begged. 'Otherwise Pantera will accuse me of helping you. Then he'll whip me.'

Juba glanced at Serapion. He was gasping and scrabbling at the edge of the tank, but the slimy fish entrails were too slippery and he fell back with a splash.

Toutis and Fronto stood by the double doors of the entrance. They had unbarred and opened them just far enough for the children to run along the earthen causeway to the main road. Ursula comforted a mewing Meer, shaken but safe.

'Tie me up!' repeated the slave boy, still on his knees.

'Use this to tie him,' Bouda thrust something into Juba's hands. It was the pretty belt of blue and gold silk that his uncle had given her.

Juba paused to glare at her, but he accepted the belt and hastily tied the boy's hands firmly behind his back. 'What's your name?'

'Claudus. They call me Claudus.'

'Will the delivery cart be here soon, Claudus?' he asked.

The boy nodded. 'It will be all right when they find me. I'll tell them the Greek tied me up.'

Juba looked down at the lame boy, now lying on his side on the warm white plaster. Then he glanced over at Serapion, who was still clinging to the edge of the tank of blood, guts and garum. 'Help me!' he cried.

Juba shook his head.

'Juba!' It was a little boy's voice.

He turned to see Audax in the gateway, hopping up and down with excitement. All the children were out, apart from him and Bouda.

As Juba started for the door, Bouda followed.

'Not you!' he snarled. 'We don't want traitors with us.'

'Please!' she begged. 'I thought that man was your friend! I didn't know! Besides,' Bouda tugged his tunic. 'I think he's drowning.'

'How can you drown in a tank of fish guts?' snorted Juba. 'It can't be that deep.'

'Then why hasn't he come out?'

Juba frowned. Serapion's head was submerged and he was no longer crying out. 'Take care of Audax!' Juba commanded Bouda. He ran to the side of the tank. The stench was so bad that he nearly retched. But he steeled himself and reached into the stew of blood and entrails. As his fingers groped for the neck of Serapion's tunic he found them closing around the Minerva cameo. Once again, anger gave him strength: he pulled so hard that it half lifted the Greek out of the water before it snapped.

Juba found he was holding the cameo and nothing else. Serapion had slipped under the surface of the garum. Everyone was gone. Only the boy lay on his side, tied up.

Should he let his enemy drown? It was a fitting way for him to go. But he remembered the words spoken to Aeneas: *Build your life upon a foundation of peace. Spare the conquered. Battle down the proud.*

'*Parcere subjectos!*' he muttered. 'Spare the conquered!'

Thrusting the cameo down the front of his tunic, he plunged his arm into the simmering fish-gut stew. He grasped a handful of hair and heaved.

Serapion flopped onto the plaster-covered floor. He was gasping and coughing.

'Whom do you worship?' Juba demanded, putting his foot on his former tutor's neck.

'What?' croaked his enemy.

'Which god or goddess do you hold dearest?'

'Isis!' Serapion exclaimed in a strangled voice. 'I worship Isis.'

'Swear on her name that you will not pursue us.'

'I . . . I swear!' he gasped. 'I promise, on the name of Isis the great mother, I will not pursue you!'

'Take me with you!' cried lame Claudus. 'Don't leave me with him if he's alive.'

'What?' Juba rounded on him. 'Now you want to come with us?'

Claudus nodded vigorously.

'All right.' Juba quickly undid his knots and used Bouda's belt to bind Serapion instead.

Serapion was on his side in a puddle of stinking fish sauce, his chest rising and falling, his eyes closed.

'Don't worry,' Juba said in Serapion's ear. There will be a salt delivery soon. They'll find you. And there's a big dog over there to keep you company.'

As he stood up, he saw the dagger lying by the side of the

tank. It was his own knife, recovered from the robbers. Juba took it and held it in front of Serapion's blinking eyes. 'If I see you again, I swear I will use this,' he warned him through gritted teeth. '*Debellare superbos!*' he growled. 'Battle down the proud!'

He slid his dagger into the special sheath on his belt.

'Come on!' he said to the slave boy.

'Wait!' Claudus beckoned him to the door of his hut. 'The children are hungry, aren't they?'

Juba nodded. 'Ravenous.'

'Every Mercury's Day they give me a week's worth of bread.' He went inside and emerged with a shoulder basket of flat round loaves.

Juba took the basket. 'Do you have water?'

The boy nodded. 'Rain barrel and a copper beaker.'

'Hard to carry,' Juba said. 'Bring the beaker. It might come in handy.' He slung the bread basket over his shoulder and went out of the hut. As he went towards the double doors, he noticed Claudus was limping again.

'Did my Uncle Pantera do that to you?' Juba asked.

'No.' The boy hung his head. 'I've had this from birth. That's why the Dark One put me out of sight.'

They closed the double doors of the fish-sauce factory. Water glittered on their left and right, but the raised track to the main road was dry.

Bouda ran to meet them. 'Juba,' she cried. 'Please forgive me! Please believe me. I didn't know that man was your enemy. He told me he was your friend.'

Juba ignored her. They had reached the main road now and turned left, so that they were heading west, with the October sun warm on their backs. The lofty poplars stood like sentinels, protecting the children from harm.

'We have bread,' cried Juba, holding up one of the leathery discs. 'But we have to get out of sight in case they come looking for us.'

He led them to a grassy spot, screened from the road by bramble bushes. Once there, he broke one of the loaves along its score and handed out the pieces.

The children happily devoured the leathery wedges of bread. Two of them ate so quickly that they got hiccups.

'Blackberries!' cried Claudus. 'I see blackberries!'

He limped over to one of the brambles and soon they were all plucking berries from the bushes and eating them greedily.

Juba leaned against a poplar and closed his eyes. 'Thank you, Genius of this place,' he whispered, 'for the rustling trees and the sweet blackberries and the clear water. Mercury, guide of travellers and merchants, guide us safely to Noviomagus and help us find a cart.'

'Juba?' Bouda tried again.

He opened his eyes and glared.

'What do you want?'

'I swear, Juba. I didn't know he was your enemy. He said he wanted to help you.' Beneath her pale blue cape she was wearing her mint-green cotton tunic from the night before and her copper hair was still in plaits. Not for the first time, he noted a blue cord around her neck.

Juba set his jaw and turned his head to watch the children. 'Tell me what happened,' he said. 'Does anyone else know we ran away?'

'No!' she cried. 'Serapion was the only one I told. I saw him walking in the portico last night, and he asked me the way to the latrines. While I was showing him, he said he was from Rome and was looking for his master's children, so that he could give them a fabulous treasure. But he told me not to tell Pantera because he might want the treasure for himself.'

Juba did not meet her gaze. He knew by now what a good liar she was and he didn't want to be fooled again. 'Why didn't you tell me last night?' he said. 'When we were all getting ready to go?'

'That was when I saw him,' she said, 'when I was on my way to the latrines. When I got back you had all gone. He said we should wait until morning. He said you wouldn't get far at night.'

'How long were you in the garum factory, waiting to surprise us?' Juba asked.

'Less than a quarter of an hour. We told Albinus that we were going for a brisk walk to balance our humours. We saw you going across the marsh and Serapion said you'd go there because the tide was coming in. He said it would be a nice surprise for you.'

Juba stood up, grasped the blue cord of her neck pouch and gave it a violent tug.

'Ow!' she cried, her hand flying to her neck.

'Juba!' cried Ursula. 'What are you doing?'

He ignored his sister and kept his gaze fixed on Bouda.

'Just because we were once rich,' he said, 'that doesn't give you permission to steal from us!'

He opened her money pouch and poured out ten silver coins.

'Look at that!' he said in mock amazement. 'Back at the Phoenix Hospitium, I gave you fifteen denarii of Domitian, all with Minerva on the back. And you still have ten left.'

'That's my money,' she said, her cheeks flaming. 'You gave it to me to get clothes and food. You didn't tell me *how* to get them.'

'So you stole the clothes and food?'

'Of course I did!' She rubbed the red mark on the back of her neck where the cord had snapped. 'What you gave me would only have bought one hooded cloak. I risked my life to get those things, so I deserve to keep this money.'

'And what about Castor? Did you lure him into that warehouse to be beaten?'

Bouda hung her head. 'Yes,' she said. 'But he was so handsome. I couldn't bear to see them beating him. They left me as a lookout while they went to the games and that's when I went to find you.'

'That explains why Tyranus is after you,' Ursula murmured. 'You betrayed him to help Castor.'

'Yes!' Bouda shot her a grateful look.

'All you care about is money!' Juba threw the coins at her feet. They rolled away like tiny silver wheels. 'You don't care about anyone or anything else!'

'I do care!' Bouda cried. 'I care about Castor and your sister and even him!' She pointed at Fronto. 'It's only you I hate!'

She bent to pick up the small silver coins.

Ursula handed her three.

'If you hate me then why are you travelling with us?' Juba demanded.

Bouda glared up at him, her green eyes brimming with tears. 'Because I don't have anybody in my life! I'm all alone. When I saw you and your brother and sister travelling on your own, I thought *I can do that too!*'

Her eyes widened as she looked over his shoulder.

Behind him, the little girls started screaming.

Juba whirled, expecting to see slimy Serapion running towards them.

But it was worse.

Chapter Fifty-One
MARGARITA

Juba's heart sank as he saw the dark rider on the black stallion.
It was his uncle Pantera.

Behind him came a white and gold carruca pulled by two snow-white oxen and driven by a chalk-white man: Albinus.

Then two riders appeared from behind the carruca: two ruddy-skinned Britons with blond moustaches.

Fool! He told himself. *Why did you let them stop to gather blackberries?*

The past twelve hours of running, hiding and shivering had been for nothing.

Audax ran to Juba and hugged his knees. Toutis and Sulinus came to stand beside him. Some of the children ran to Fronto, others to Ursula. He noticed that none of them went to Bouda.

As they jostled him from behind, he remembered how he had sheltered them like puppies the night before. In that moment, Juba knew he would do anything to make sure these children were not taken captive again.

As Pantera rode forward, Juba stood his ground. His uncle was wearing a tunic of fine black wool, and over it a breastplate of black iron with a brass Medusa head at its centre. His short cloak was black and so were his boots.

The paleness of the bodyguards with their long blond moustaches and tunics of cream linen made his uncle seem even blacker.

The Dark One, the children had called him. He dresses like that to frighten people, thought Juba. *I will not show fear.*

But it was hard not to flinch as Pantera rode so close that Juba could feel the horse's hot breath on his face. His uncle looked down at him with cold eyes. 'I offer you hospitality and this is how you thank me? By fleeing with my property like thieves in the night?'

Juba made his hands into fists. 'They're not your property!' he said. 'They're all freeborn children. I'm taking them back to their families.' He tried to sound brave but he could hear his voice quavering.

'I bought them.' His uncle's voice was ice cold. 'I paid for them in gold. They belong to me.'

'They were kidnapped,' Juba took a step back so his uncle's horse wouldn't tread on Audax, still clinging like a limpet. 'They weren't yours to buy.'

'And yet I did buy them.' His uncle's saddle creaked as he shifted in it. 'I paid a thousand sesterces for each of them. That is twelve thousand sesterces in all. And if I sell them in Rome, the profit will be ten times what I paid.'

'Is that all you care about?' Juba said. 'Profit?'

'I care about profit,' said his uncle, 'so that I can look after my household. My family and slaves,' he added.

What family? Juba thought. But he did not say it. Instead he took a deep breath. 'Have you heard of the Pearl of Iris, my father's most valuable gem? He told me it is more valuable than both our villas put together.'

Above him, his uncle gave a single nod. 'Of course I've heard of it. It is worth a fortune.'

'Will you accept that gem in return for the children?'

His uncle raised an eyebrow. 'You want to buy them back?'

'Yes. I want to redeem them.'

'Then you are no better than I am.'

'I'm not going to keep them as slaves,' Juba's anger helped him overcome his fear. 'I'm going to take them back to their families.'

His uncle snorted. 'You don't even know where they're from.'

'Yes, I do. They're from a place called Aquae Sulis.'

'Which is a hundred miles from here.' His uncle shook his head. 'Do you really have the Pearl of Iris?'

'Yes.'

Pantera dismounted. Juba was eye to eye with the brass Medusa on his iron breastplate. The Gorgon was grinning and sticking her tongue out at him.

'Where is it?' his uncle said.

Juba pointed. 'Behind that tree. Wait here.'

'You're going to run away.'

'I won't run away,' Juba said fiercely. 'I wouldn't abandon my brother and sister. Or these children. Wait here.'

His uncle raised his eyebrows. 'Very well.'

Juba gently pried Audax's arms from around his knees and whispered, 'Wait here with Fronto and the others. I'll be right back.'

He went past the nearest poplar tree into the woods. Once out of sight he felt the seam of his cloak.

Had his revelation in the garum factory been right? He had not even tested it. As he felt his way along the seams, he remembered how his mother had patted his chest.

This is your father's birrus Britannicus, worth a fortune. He told you its secret, didn't he?

And he remembered all those times he thought he was lying on pebbles.

At last his trembling fingers felt something inside the seam where the hood was attached to the cape. Taking his dagger from its sheath, he cut two stitches. As he used his thumbs to work the object up and out, he wondered if his mother had made those stitches herself when she sewed his father's gems into the seams of the cloak.

The crack of a twig nearby made him freeze, and a bird flew up out of some shrubs. He held his breath and continued to work at the seam.

A bright object fell onto the ground and lay on the damp earth between blades of grass. It was like a chickpea, gleaming pale pink in the morning light.

Juba held it in the palm of his right hand and emerged from behind the tree.

He kept the pearl clenched in his fist as he walked to his uncle.

'Do I have your word that you will let us go?'

His uncle nodded coldly. 'Because you are my brother's children,' he said. 'I swear by Jupiter Ammon that I will not pursue you or the children nor do you any harm. Albinus here is my witness.'

He looked towards the carriage and Albinus nodded his assent.

'Will you also let us have the carriage and oxen?' Juba asked. 'So I can take these children home?'

His uncle's mouth twitched. He was not looking at Juba, but staring up the road.

'Very well,' his uncle said at last. 'You may have the carruca. But not my driver. Not Albinus.'

Juba realised he had asked far too little for the Pearl of Iris. This gave him courage.

'Furthermore,' Juba continued, 'you must promise not to buy or sell slaves ever again.'

'How dare you!' His uncle rounded on him and Juba took an involuntary step backwards.

'The Pearl of Iris is worth ten thousand slaves,' Juba said stoutly. 'Besides,' he added. 'You must make a huge profit on the garum you make here in Britannia.'

His uncle's jaw dropped. 'How do you know about that?'

'We've just seen it,' Juba said. 'We added a secret ingredient to the mixture.'

'You are not to tell anyone about that!'

'And you are not to buy or sell people.'

'I could have you killed. I could do it myself.' His uncle hissed. 'I could throttle you right here, right now.'

'But you wouldn't,' Juba hoped his uncle couldn't detect fear. 'Because you just made a solemn vow to Jupiter Ammon.'

His uncle clenched his jaw. 'Very well. Give me the pearl.'

'No, Juba!' cried Ursula. 'Don't trust him!'

'I have to trust him,' Juba said. 'There's no other way.'

Juba held out his fist, turned it and opened his hand.

His uncle's eyes widened a fraction. Then he regained control and made his expression blank. He took the pearl and studied it. Finally he reached behind his iron breastplate and into the neck of his tunic. He pulled out a small black pouch on a leather thong. He slipped the Pearl of Iris inside.

'Go,' he said, looking at Juba, Fronto and Ursula in turn. 'Go and never come back.'

Then he looked at Bouda and smiled. 'You, however, may stay with me in my palace as an honoured guest. I can promise you a room of your own with a feather mattress and fur covers. I will dress you in soft cotton and glittering jewels. I could use a resourceful child like you,' he added. 'An innocent-looking girl who appreciates luxury and the finer things in life. Will you come back to Fishbrook with me, Bouda?'

Chapter Fifty-Two
CARRUCA

Ursula's stomach flipped like a beached fish when her uncle smiled at Bouda.

He didn't want them, but he wanted *her*? She felt a strange pang of jealousy.

But Bouda was looking at Juba. 'Shall I go with him?'

Juba did not reply.

'You don't trust me, do you?'

Juba shook his head. 'No. Not really.'

'So you don't mind if I go to live with your uncle?'

'Of course I mind!'

'Then do you want me to come with you?'

Juba turned away from her, his jaw clenched.

'Juba, tell her!' cried Ursula. 'Tell her to stay with us.'

He did not reply so Ursula said it: 'Please come with us, Bouda. It wouldn't be the same without you.' Meer mewed on her shoulder. 'See? Meer wants you too!'

Fronto looked up from under his eyebrows. '*I'd* like you to stay,' he said.

Bouda gave him a half smile, which faded as she looked back at Juba. He was still silent.

'Juba!' Ursula hissed, 'what would Aeneas do?'

Juba gave a bitter laugh. 'Aeneas abandoned Dido because he had a mission,' he said. 'He knew she would distract him from it.' Then he took a deep breath.

'Bouda, don't come with us unless you mean it,' he said. 'For the next few days we'll be wanderers. I can promise nights on the cold, hard earth and travel-stained cloaks as your blanket. Roast squirrel and stale bread will be your food. The sky will be our ceiling and the road our floor. We'll get wet and hungry. But we'll be doing something noble,' he rested his hand lightly on Ursula's non-kitten shoulder. 'We have a mission. Like Aeneas.'

Ursula turned to Bouda. 'I used to like dangerous Turnus more than dutiful Aeneas,' she said. 'But I was wrong. Turnus is good for exciting stories, but in real life you want Aeneas.'

Suddenly little Velvinna left Ursula's side and ran to Bouda and hugged her legs. 'Come with us?' she lifted her blackberry stained face. 'Please?'

Bouda stared at Juba.

'Do you even like me?' she whispered, her green eyes swimming with unshed tears. Ursula held her breath. She knew the question was for Juba and him alone.

Juba sighed. 'Yes, Bouda' he said. 'I may not trust you, but I like you very much.'

Bouda gave a faltering smile. 'All right,' she said. 'I'll come with you.'

The children cheered. With a grunt of disgust, Pantera swung onto his horse and kicked the stallion into a gallop. One of his bodyguards set off after him; the other stopped to let Albinus mount behind him.

Chapter Fifty-Three
PRODIGIUM

As Juba watched his uncle ride away he was aware of arms hugging his leg. 'Lift,' said Audax.

Juba bent down and picked up the little boy.

'Lift,' repeated Audax, pointing a chubby finger towards the carruca.

'Yes,' he said. 'We have to give you a lift to Londinium. Flavia Gemina will be overjoyed to see you, and your parents, too.

'Lift,' said Audax.

'I think he wants to ride on an ox,' said Ursula.

'Not a good idea!' Juba smiled, but he took Audax over to let him stroke the oxen. They were huge but had gentle eyes.

The other children were now swarming in and around the carruca, investigating their transport and shelter for the next few days. Ursula came to stand beside Juba and Audax. She stroked the other ox. 'I'm going to call them Volens and Dignus,' she said. 'Willing and Worthy.'

Juba looked down at her. 'Thank you,' he said.

'Why?' Ursula was stroking Volens' nose.

'For what you said. About me being like Aeneas. That means a lot to me.'

She turned from the oxen to face him. 'Juba, I think you are

214

very brave. It must have been hard for you to do what you did in Ostia. Leaving Dora with that woman. But you knew what we didn't: that Mater and Pater were never coming to get her.'

'Do you forgive me?'

'Yes, especially since I had to leave Loquax behind when we fled with the children. It was the hardest decision I've ever had to make.'

Her eyes were full of tears and he put his free arm round her to give her a squeeze. She hugged him back, but Audax squirmed in Juba's arms and pushed her head away. Then he pointed at the ox. 'Lift!'

They both laughed.

'It's a good-sized travelling carriage,' Fronto said, coming up to them. 'It has two long benches and some plain canvas cushions. I think most of the little ones will fit inside. And these look like fine oxen.' He tapped their foreheads and murmured *right, left, right.*

Juba put Audax down on the road and called out. 'Hey! Does anybody know how to feed these things?'

'I do,' offered a boy who could not have been more than eight. 'My papa has an ox cart. He delivers things. I can even drive it!'

'What's your name?' Ursula asked him.

'Sulinus.'

Juba frowned and looked at another boy. 'I thought you were called Sulinus?'

'I am.'

'Me, too,' said another boy.

Juba grinned at the boy who claimed he could drive an ox-cart. 'We'll call you Sulinus Bubulus, which is Latin for having to do with oxen.'

Sulinus Bubulus nodded happily and started to clamber up to the seat. Little Audax tried to follow him.

'Wait!' cried Fronto. 'We have to ask the gods to bless us.'

'Yes,' Juba grabbed Audax again and hoisted him up, even though his arms were aching. 'Everybody! Gather round.'

They formed a semi-circle around the two oxen.

Juba looked around at the children. 'We are going to drive this fine carriage to the great town of Londinium, and then we will take you home!'

Some of the children cheered. Juba made a patting motion for silence.

'Before we set out,' he said, 'we want to ask our gods to protect us on our journey.' He put up the hood of his tunic and turned to Fronto. 'You're the eldest,' he said. 'Do you want to ask the gods' blessing?'

Fronto smiled. He covered his head with his hood and placed both hands on the oxen.

Ursula put two fingers lightly on Meer's head, to bless her, too. The kitten purred.

'Jupiter, king of the gods,' Fronto prayed. 'If you see us safely to Londinium and then to Aquae Sulis, I vow that we will sacrifice one of these fine—'

'No!' cried Ursula. 'Not the oxen. I've given them names!'

Momentarily confused, Fronto looked at Juba.

'Altar,' Juba mouthed the word. 'Vow an altar.'

Fronto nodded. 'If you see us safely to Londinium and then to Aquae Sulis, we vow to dedicate a marble altar as thanks. Please give us a sign that you will be with us.'

Everyone stood very quietly, looking up into the sky and waiting for a sign.

As if on cue, a bird fluttered down out of a nearby tree and onto Ursula's shoulder. '*Carpe diem!*' said Loquax. '*Carpe diem!*'

The children laughed and cheered, Ursula loudest of all.

Suddenly Audax cried, 'Mama!'

Juba looked up to see a familiar mule-cart driving towards them. Mulio the driver was in the middle. On his left sat Flavia Gemina, all in sky blue. On his right sat a slim young woman with dark skin and a mustard yellow stola. Even as Mulio reined in the cart, the woman in yellow was scrambling down and now she was running towards them.

'Audax!' she cried. 'My Audax!'

Juba lowered the squirming toddler to the ground and he was off and running, his bare feet slapping the paved road.

Audax and his mother met in the middle of the road and she spun him around, sobbing and laughing at the same time.

Juba swallowed hard and blinked back tears.

'As far as signs go,' he said. 'I think those will do.'

Chapter Fifty-Four
EXQUAESTORES

They were halfway to Venta Belgarum when it began to get dark.

It was such a mild night that they decided to camp in a clearing beside the road. They sat on shared cloaks and blankets around a crackling fire. Silver birch trees and a brook sheltered them on one side and the two carriages on the other. The four mules and the two oxen had been fed and stabled at a nearby inn. And the inn had provided bread, cheese and warm spiced wine for their dinner.

They had eaten and drunk their fill. Now the fire warmed their hands and faces. Audax was snuggled next to his mother while Flavia Gemina was explaining why she had left her children to find them.

'Seeing you children with the soldiers reminded me of the days when Nubia and I were girls.' She exchanged a fond look with her friend. 'What adventures we had! There was tragedy and death, but we saved many children.' She looked at Juba. 'You reminded me of all that.'

The flames crackled and Fronto leaned forward to put another two branches on the fire.

'After I put you on Mulio's cart,' Flavia said, 'I was restless.

My mind was working the way it used to. I began to ask some of the governor's clerks about your uncle. One of them had a friend whose cousin comes from this region. He said the local people's nickname for Pantera is the Dark One. Then your pigeon arrived, with his ribbon still on but no message. I knew you might be in danger, so Nubia and I set out at once . . .'

Nubia squeezed Audax and kissed the top of his head.

'We were almost at Fishbrook,' said Flavia Gemina, 'when our axle broke and we had to spend the night at an inn.'

Two of the British girls had come to sit beside her and she had her arms around them. Compared to their gold hair, hers seemed brown. *The same colour as Mater's*, Juba thought. *And her eyes are the same clear grey.*

'When we asked if they knew of the Dark One, they told us about your brief visit yesterday.'

'The Blue Cockerel Inn!' said Juba. 'I hope they didn't spit on you.'

'They were wary at first,' said Flavia, 'but when the girl understood that we wanted to help she told us all she could.'

Flavia Gemina sat forward. 'The gods helped you find little Audax, just in time. But there are many other children in this province who have gone missing. Important men do not care about them, but we do.' Here she clasped her friend's hand. Then she looked at Juba.

'This morning, when you spoke of doing something noble – like Aeneas – it inspired me. Yes!' she laughed at his look of surprise. 'I heard the whole encounter! We saw someone who could only be the Dark One with his bodyguards riding west, and I told Nubia and Mulio to wait. I crept into the woods to hear what he had to say. You almost found me,' she added, 'when you went behind a tree to get the treasure from your cloak.'

'So you know,' he said, 'what kind of person my uncle is?'

Flavia nodded. 'More importantly, I know what kind of person *you* are. What you said – about being wanderers, sleeping rough and enduring wind and rain to help others – it inspired me! We can find other lost children once we have returned these to their parents. It would be a dangerous task, but also an exciting one.'

'Should we adopt new names?' asked Ursula.

'Keep the names you have now,' said Flavia looking at each of them fondly. 'They suit you well. But perhaps you can each come up with a false name, in case you are questioned. Use my name as your nomen but choose your own cognomen.'

'My secret cognomen will be Felina!' cried Ursula. 'Flavia Felina.'

'I'll be Aeneas,' said Juba and Fronto together. Everybody laughed but Juba felt a pang, almost like the loss of a friend. It was Aeneas who had kept him going in the hardest moments.

'Let's toss a coin,' suggested Fronto.

'Or,' said Flavia, looking at Fronto. 'You could be Latinus, the wise king who correctly understands signs and portents. That way Juba can be Aeneas.'

'Yes,' said Fronto. 'I'll be Lucius Flavius Latinus and I'll let Juba be Aeneas.'

'Thank you,' said Juba to Fronto, and he nodded his gratitude to Flavia, who nodded back.

Bouda shyly raised her hand.

'Yes, Bouda?' said Flavia.

'May I be a quester, too?' she asked. 'And may I have the secret name Flavia Vulpa?'

'What a good secret cognomen!' Flavia Gemina clapped her

hands. 'And what a wonderful name for our little guild: the Questers of Britannia.'

Flavia looked at Juba. 'What shall we do with these children whose parents are missing them?' she asked.

He smiled at her. 'Take them home,' he said.

'And when will we do that?' she said.

'Tomorrow,' he said, looking at his brother and sister and Bouda. Then he looked at the children. 'In a few days, if the gods are willing, we will be back in your village. And there will be great rejoicing.'

FINIS

WHAT THE LATIN CHAPTER
HEADERS MEAN

1. BIRRUS – cloak
   A long woollen cloak with a hood; they were especially popular in Britannia

2. LUCERNA – lamp
   A clay or metal vessel filled with oil or fat that fed a flaming wick

3. AMPHORAE – large storage jars
   Their many different shapes showed where they were from and what they held

4. AENEAS – the name of a Trojan hero
   The poet Virgil tells his story in a great epic poem called The Aeneid

5. AQUAE DUCTUM – aqueduct
   A channel for bringing water into town, often elevated on high arches

6. CIRCUS MAXIMUS – hippodrome
   The great racecourse of Rome was one of its most famous landmarks

7. PORTA OSTIENSIS – the Ostia Gate
   This arch in Rome's massive Servian wall led to the seaports of Ostia and Portus

8. NECROPOLIS – graveyard
   Greek for 'city of the dead'; Roman graveyards were always outside town walls

9. GEMMA – gemstone
    Today we call a gem with a carved profile portrait a 'cameo'

10. DAEMON – demon
    A spirit or supernatural being which was considered harmful or evil

11. PLAUSTRUM – wagon
    A sturdy four-wheeled vehicle for carrying heavy loads

12. COLUMBARIUM – tomb
    A building with niches for funeral urns

13. CINERARIA – urns
    Glass or clay jars held the ashes and bones of cremated bodies

14. INSULA – apartment block
    Roman apartment blocks often had several stories around an inner courtyard

15. CUPAE – barrels
    In addition to amphorae, wooden casks were also used for transporting liquids

16. NAVIS – ship
    In Roman times, travellers had to book passage on merchant ships

17. BRASSICA – cabbage
    Cabbage was a cheap and popular food in Roman times

18. VIRGA – cane
    Birch rods were commonly used to punish schoolboys and slaves

19. OCEANUS – the Atlantic Ocean
The great sea of water that surrounded the known world

20. PANIS NAUTICUS – ship's biscuit
Made of flour and water plus a little lard and salt, this hard tack lasted for weeks

21. MATELLA – chamberpot
Sailors peed over the side of the ship or used buckets, but rich passengers and women would bring a chamberpot

22. DUBRIS – Dover
With its famous white cliffs, Dover was Britannia's closest point to Gaul (France)

23. RUTUPIAE – Richborough
Claudius launched his invasion of Britannia from this port in AD 43

24. LONDINIUM – London
Lower Thames Street marks the northern shoreline of the river in Roman times

25. DOLIUM – wide-mouthed storage jar
This type of massive clay pot was big enough for a man to fit inside

26. HOSPITIUM – inn
Lodging-houses in Roman times ranged from basic to luxurious

27. MILITES – soldiers
Roman soldiers performed many functions in addition to fighting

28. PATINA – egg flan
An ancient dish like a modern quiche to which almost anything could be added

29. PRAETORIUM – palace
The commander's house in a fortress or a governor's palace in a town

30. PRINCEPS – Emperor
A term meaning 'first citizen' which Roman emperors applied to themselves

31. MULIO – mule-driver
Mules and oxen were the most popular animals for pulling heavy loads

32. MANSIO – official inn
Run by the central government, these were mainly for officials and messengers

33. STRIGILIS – scraper
A dull bronze or silver blade used to remove dirt, sweat and oil from the body

34. OLEUM – olive-oil
Oil had many functions, including as a gentle skin cleanser and perfume

35. FAX – torch
Outdoor lighting was mainly from wood dipped in pine-pitch and set alight

36. BACULUM – walking stick
A staff used as a support in walking

37. COHORS – cohort
A unit of soldiers, usually about five hundred men

38. PARDALOCAMP – sea-panther
A mythical sea-monster, part leopard and part fish

39. STATUA – sculpture
Marble statues were often painted to make them look as realistic as possible

40. TRICLINIUM – dining space
Some rich Romans reclined on three couches for formal dinner parties

41. PROCURATOR – important official
This official supervised taxation, army salaries and income from imperial properties

42. CATENAE – chains
Chains for slaves have been found in Roman Britain as well as Pompeii

43. CLAVIS – key
Roman keys were made of bronze or iron

44. DAMA – deer
Bones of imported fallow deer have been found at Fishbourne Roman Palace

45. HORREUM – storehouse
Roman forts often built granaries on stilts to keep the grain dry and pest-free

46. TENEBRAE – darkness
Romans associated darkness with sleep, ignorance and death

47. PALUS – swamp
The area south of Fishbourne Roman Palace was swampy in Roman times

48. CANIS – dog
The hollow shape of a guard dog was found in the hardened ash of Pompeii

49. GARUM – fish-sauce
A seasoning made of salted fish blood and guts, a little like Worcestershire Sauce

50. CINGULUM – belt
Roman belts could be made of leather, cloth or metal

51. MARGARITA – pearl
Julius Caesar once paid six million sesterces for a single pearl

52. CARRUCA – coach
These luxury Roman travelling carriages often had benches and windows

53. PRODIGIUM – omen
Romans looked for signs and portents in weather and behaviour of birds

54. EXQUAESTORES – seekers
This is invented: there was no department of missing persons in ancient Rome

The adventure continues in the second
Roman Quest, coming in October 2016.